Terror

In a state of panic, Lucy swung round at the same time as a ghastly white figure appeared in the doorway. She froze in terror as the eyes seemed to bore into her flesh. A faint stench, as of rotting flesh, filled her nostrils. . . .

The woman advanced toward her. Suddenly a wave of blistering heat passed through Lucy's body, turning her blood to molten lava and her heart to a cauldron about to erupt.

Lucy lost consciousness.

point

All on a Winter's Day

Lisa Taylor

SCHOLASTIC INC.
New York Toronto London Auckland Sydney

ISBN 0-590-43416-0

Copyright © 1989 by Lisa Taylor. All rights reserved. Published by Scholastic Inc., 730 Broadway, New York, NY 10003, by arrangement with Scholastic Publications Ltd., United Kingdom. POINT is a registered trademark of Scholastic Inc.

12 11 10 9 8 7 6 5 4 3 2 1   0 1 2 3 4 5/9

Printed in the U.S.A.   01

First Scholastic printing, November 1990

For Mum and Dad
with love

Chapter One

It was in the early hours of the morning that Lucy awoke. She sat up with a start. She was so cold that she could have been outside. Her clothes were soaking wet where the perspiration had soaked through. She had had a nightmare. At least, she thought that was what it was. In those brief moments between sleeping and waking, Lucy had forgotten the precise details of her dream. Only the terror remained and the fleeting sensation of someone, or something, pulling her down.

The room was strangely quiet. Lucy realized that the clock had stopped. It was the first time in three years – since she had been given it as a Christmas present. Now the still hours remained ominously unbroken by its ticking. The only sound to pierce the silence was the thumping of Lucy's heart.

Through the window Lucy watched the moon emerge from behind a cloud, bathing the room in a phosphorescent glow and throwing strange warped shadows about the walls. It seemed to transform everything it touched. Wherever she looked, Lucy saw once familiar objects in a ghastly unfamiliar light, or as mere outlines of ghostly forms. Over by the door, instead of a dressing gown, there now hung the twisted, headless figure of a man. And from the top of a bookshelf a much-hugged teddy bear gazed menacingly down, as if reproaching Lucy for the half-dismembered body which was the heavy toll of a child's careless love.

Suddenly Lucy saw a dark shape, silhouetted against the pale winter sky, pass across the window and disappear into an unlit recess of the room.

"Hugh?" she whispered, half afraid that her voice would not penetrate the gloom. "Hugh? Is that you?" The blackness loomed up at her and offered no reply. Then came her brother's small voice:

"I woke up and I couldn't breathe. It was as if someone was strangling me. It's so cold. Lucy . . . I'm scared."

Lucy drew such a sharp intake of breath that it whistled through her teeth. Hugh, of the conker-coloured hair and three hundred and forty-nine freckles! Hugh, Champion Chinese Burner and British Bulldog King! Hugh, whose only fear up until now was that somebody would find out his second name was Cecil! It was hard to believe that he had enough sense to be scared.

"Come on," said Lucy quietly. "We'll go and find Mum." Lucy groped her way over towards the door and grabbed a dressing gown off the hook. She chucked one over to Hugh.

"Here! Put these on," she said, handing him a pair of slippers and pulling on her own. She fumbled around for the door handle. She was so cold that even

2

the touch of metal against her skin felt warm. She twisted the handle first one way, then the other, and finally tried to force it using both hands at once. It was as if somebody was holding it from outside.

"Hugh!" she whispered. "I can't open the door!" From somewhere out of the murky shadows, Hugh emerged to grab the handle. It clicked and turned and the door swung noiselessly open.

"Puny Marooney!" whispered Hugh, objectionable even in adversity. But he still felt for Lucy's hand before going through the door. It was an entirely new experience for Lucy, holding her brother's hand. She was surprised to find that it was even colder than her own – and so clammy that it could have been dipped in water.

Outside in the corridor the darkness was unrelieved. There were no windows here for the moonlight to filter through. Lucy was uncertain which was worse – the sinister shadows of the half-light or the blackness of the complete unknown. Lucy reached for the light switch. The light wasn't working. She was glad that her brother had turned softy enough to hold her hand.

Suddenly her arm was wrenched nearly from its socket. There was a muffled thump followed by a sharp cry.

"Who moved that table?" hissed Hugh from the floor. Lucy wanted to giggle but she was afraid of what it would sound like in the dark. Typical Hugh – blaming everyone else.

At last they reached their mother's bedroom. As she groped for the handle, Lucy half expected it not to turn. But this time the door seemed to open almost as soon as she touched it. Inside, the room was as dark as the corridor. The curtains were drawn.

"Mum!" called Hugh. "Mum! Don't worry. It's only us!" There was no reply.

"Mum?" Still no reply.

"Switch on the light," whispered Lucy. Hugh flicked the switch but nothing happened.

"There must be a power cut," she said. "Hugh, you're nearer the window. Pull the curtains back." There were a few fumbling noises as Hugh located the window, then a swish as the curtains were pulled back. Immediately the room was filled with an eerie light.

Lucy squinted as her eyes became accustomed to the change and the room took on a blurred impression. She blinked hard several times. The first thing that occurred to her was that the bed was empty. The next was that it was actually in a different place. The third was that the bed itself was different. And after that, so many things occurred to her in so short a space of time that it would be impossible to put them in any order. In a few brief moments, Lucy realized that the whole room was different – not just the way it was arranged, but the things which were actually in it. Over by the window Hugh was moaning audibly. Lucy thought she was going to scream.

"Come on!" she yelled. "Let's get out of here!" and in seconds they were both out of the door.

Chapter Two

It was no mere coincidence that Hugh had fallen over once before. As they stumbled wildly towards the stairs, it became apparent that the furniture in the corridor had also changed. Lucy drew a deep breath and grabbed her brother by the arm.

"We've got to go slowly, Hugh," she hissed. "Otherwise we'll end up getting hurt." It was the hardest thing that Lucy had ever done. While her heart thumped so heavily that she could hardly breathe, while her whole frame shook with a fear that she had never known before, while all her being vibrated with the sense that she should run, and run as fast as she could, Lucy crept along the corridor, holding her brother's hand. For even greater than her desire to run was the fear that she might fall and, unable to get up, be left victim to whatever she imagined was behind. So on she crept, up the corridor and down the stairs, gripped by her brother and by a dread that made her blood run cold.

"What about Mum?" whispered Hugh. He was shivering violently. Lucy wondered whether it was the cold, or the fear, or both.

"I don't think she can be here," replied Lucy. She didn't want to start thinking about where her mother could be. She was near to hysteria as it was. Together they inched their way further through the house, sometimes creeping, sometimes crawling, fumbling blindly, for ever slow, and all the while two words kept hammering over and over in Lucy's head: GET OUT! GET OUT!

At last they came to the front door. As Hugh reached for the handle, Lucy wondered again whether it would stick like before. It did. She gasped.

"It's only the latch," whispered Hugh. Lucy heaved a shaky sigh of relief. With the latch released, the door creaked open and a chill blast swept through the house.

Outside, the pale grey sky hung heavy with the promise of more snow. On the ground it was already several inches thick. Straight ahead, Lucy could just make out the outline of the gate. And to her left the frozen surface of the lake glittered like crystal in the moonshine. It sent an extra shudder down Lucy's spine. She didn't know why. Far off, a wild animal's night call echoed mockingly across the marsh. Lucy thought it sounded like a woman crying.

"Where are we going?" called Hugh, as they started racing towards the gate.

"To Mrs Latter's," Lucy called back. "It's the nearest." Mrs Latter was their closest neighbour. But she still lived two miles across the marsh. And Lucy wasn't at all sure she could find her way in the dark. But there was very little alternative. Anything was better than staying in the house.

A few metres ahead of her, Hugh had already opened the gate. Even from where she was, Lucy could hear his teeth chattering with the cold.

"Hurry!" he yelled. She ran as fast as she could. When she got there, Hugh was still standing in the same place.

"Well, go on!" she cried. "What are you waiting for?" But Hugh just stood there, numb and expressionless, his arms hanging limply by his sides.

"I can't go through," he said. Lucy softened. He was just scared.

"Come on," she said gently, taking him once more by the hand. "I'll go first," and she turned to lead the way. But as soon as she got to the opening, something stopped her. Nothing hard or soft particularly. But something indescribable – like a vacuum, which sucked her up and locked her body in a state of frozen animation, beyond which it was impossible to move. She stepped back and tried again. It was no use.

Lucy felt the panic rise like a bubble in her chest and threaten to burst. She swallowed hard and forced the bubble back down.

"We'll go further round!" she yelled and started off in the opposite direction to the lake. But wherever they went the same thing happened. It was like a barrier, running all the way round the edge of the grounds.

For the second time that night, Lucy wanted to scream. She wanted to cry out, to surrender herself to the terrible hysteria which lurked just below the surface of her control. Instead, she gritted her teeth and clenched her fists and tried to maintain her composure.

"Lift me up!" shouted Hugh. Lucy stared at him.

"Lift me up! If it's like a wall, then we might be able to get over the top."

7

So Lucy struggled to lift Hugh on to her shoulders. But when he got there, he found he couldn't even straighten up his back. Whatever was stopping them appeared to be in the shape of a dome, curving inwards and encircling the house.

"What do we do now?" asked Hugh. The chattering of his teeth rang out like an alarm bell through the cold night air. It was clear that they couldn't stay outside. Lucy shivered from her head to the tips of her toes.

"We'll have to go back inside the house," she said.

Chapter Three

From where she was standing, the house looked bigger than Lucy remembered it – a dark, faceless mass which towered out of the sparkling, snow-covered ground as if it was a mountain waiting to be conquered. The night had stripped it of all character and form. Gone were the ochre-washed brick and the white-painted windows; gone was the grand old porch with its inscription and the carvings underneath; gone was the brilliant red and green of the creeper which clamoured about the door and up the walls. All had disappeared beneath a grey and uniform gloom, so Lucy could imagine that everything had changed under its cover.

Lucy hugged herself tight, took a last deep breath and started heading back towards the house. Hugh followed, several paces behind. There was no sound save the wind as it swept across the marshland, whipping up the snow and lashing it round and about the children's heads. They were so numb with cold that they hardly noticed the sting as it struck their faces.

Suddenly Lucy realized that Hugh was no longer behind her. As she turned to look she could see him, about fifty metres back, crouched in the snow in an attempt to shelter himself from the bitter night wind. The air, which streamed from his mouth like smoke, showed that he was breathing very heavily.

"What's wrong?" shouted Lucy, surprised at the shrillness of her voice. She saw Hugh straighten himself to answer, but as the wind whipped up and carried off his reply, she caught only the faintest impression of an anguished cry. She trudged back to where he was.

"What's wrong, Hugh?" she said, bending down so that she was on a level with her brother.

"I'm not going back inside the house," hissed Hugh. "Not without Mum!" Lucy exhaled sharply and her breath formed a cloud in the air.

"But we've got to go back in," she insisted gently. "Look at us! We'll freeze to death out here."

"Where is she, Lucy? What's happened?"

"I don't know," said Lucy. "I don't understand it either. But I do know that Mum wouldn't just leave us. She's got to be around here somewhere. Now come on." And with that she coaxed Hugh back on to his feet. "I'm sure it'll turn out all right in the end," she said and together they started to retrace their steps towards the house.

The light was beginning very gradually to change. Lucy felt her spirits rise by the smallest degree. Not for any particular reason. Perhaps it was the onset of the dawn and the promise of a new day. Or perhaps it was the mere knowledge that the night was going to end. As they got nearer to the house, Lucy could detect faint traces of the red and green of the creeper as it penetrated the lifting gloom and, nearer still, the yellow wash of the brickwork. She heaved a sigh of relief. At least everything outside had remained the same.

Hardly faltering, Lucy guided Hugh up to the porch and through the doorway. Immediately they were plunged back into darkness. But it was no longer the pitch black of the dead of night. Now they could dimly discern the outlines of strange, unfamiliar objects and were able to negotiate a safe passage in between.

"Where are we going?" whispered Hugh.

"To our bedroom," Lucy whispered back. It was like a last place of sanctuary – the only room in the whole house which she was certain had not changed.

Just as they got to the foot of the stairs, there was a sharp click as of a door shutting in the corridor above, followed by the soft pad of footsteps across the floor. Instantly, Lucy grabbed Hugh and pulled him down behind the bannister.

For a few seconds more there was silence. Then the patter of footsteps started again. They were quiet and very light and so regular that you could almost have kept time to them, except that every now and then there was a slight change of rhythm, as the sound of one step seemed to fall fractionally after the other. Then, very swiftly, they would resume their monotonous beat.

From where they were hiding, Lucy and Hugh could hear the footsteps getting nearer. There was a momentary pause as they reached the top of the stairs, then a sudden change of rhythm as they started to descend them. There was an awful inevitability about the sound – like a metronome accompanying a silent tune. You knew it would carry on beating to the end. What you didn't know was when the end would be.

Lucy squeezed herself round and pressed her face close against the railings of the bannister. Through the gaps she could just about see halfway up the stairs. She was faced with a horrible choice. Either she could close her eyes and leave to her imagination the horrors that lay behind those footsteps. Or she could see for herself. Lucy could only hope that the darkness and the fact that she was crouched so low, would prevent whatever it was from seeing her. She cast a quick sideways glance towards her brother. His eyes were open too.

Glancing back, Lucy just managed to stifle a fearful cry as she saw two tiny pairs of feet appear simultaneously on the stairs. She watched in horrible fascination as the rest of the figures came completely into view. Frail, fragile figures with coal-black hair and deep dark eyes, and skin which could have been made out of china it was so delicate and white. Two children, a boy and a girl, younger than Lucy and Hugh – about six or seven years of age – clad in long, pale gowns and so similar that they had to be twins. They moved in effortless unison, gliding as if in a trance, their hands clasped together in an attitude of prayer, their eyes wide and vacant, registering nothing of the outside world. Their beautiful faces, which were expressionless apart from a slight furrowing about their brows, gave them an aspect of worried bewilderment. As they passed, Lucy felt a deep sense of sadness and despair. She wanted to leap up and stop them. She wanted to remove all their doubt and all their fear. But something warned her against it.

"Stop!" cried Hugh, jumping up and waving his arms. "Stop! Don't go!" But it seemed the children did not hear him. Hugh started to chase after them.

"Hugh! Don't!" shouted Lucy. But she was too late. Hugh had already caught them up.

"We'll help you!" he cried, as he put out his arm to stop them. But his hand passed straight through their bodies and the children moved heedlessly on across the hall.

Chapter Four

When Lucy reached Hugh, he was still in the same position, fixed in a posture of disbelief, his arm outstretched towards the retreating figures as they gradually disappeared down the passageway. His whole frame shook violently. His usually ruddy face was drained, devoid of colour – even the freckles had gone. Suddenly it didn't seem possible that he was only ten years old.

"It . . . it went straight through," he murmured. "My hand – it went straight through their bodies!"

"I know," said Lucy.

"I only wanted to help them, Lucy . . . they looked so real."

"I wanted to help them too," she said. She felt suddenly ashamed.

"They were so sad. So frightened. Nobody should be like that."

"Come on," said Lucy, glancing nervously around. "We must get back to the bedroom. I don't think it's safe out here."

Together they moved past the unknown furniture and mysterious forms which now imprinted rather clearer impressions upon the rising twilight. Back across the hall to where they had crouched, half hidden behind the bannister, then on up the stairs, their steps less regular, more urgent, than those which had recently descended them. Along the corridor to the bedroom and the door, which clicked sharply open. It was the same sound as had announced the presence of those other unearthly souls. Lucy wondered from which room the ghostly steps had come.

Inside the bedroom everything remained unchanged. If there had been any visitors they had left no outward signs. Automatically, Lucy locked the door and removed the key. Hugh looked at her with vague uncertainty. She knew what he was thinking: solid wood was small protection against the insubstantial threat of human shadows. But for Lucy the door stood like a division between two worlds – one real and familiar, the other shady and unknown. And it was the fear of their entanglement that Lucy wanted to shut out.

"W-what shall we do now?" asked Hugh.

Lucy looked at her brother in alarm. He could hardly speak he was shivering so badly and his whole frame was convulsed in violent tremors. Lucy was hardly in a better state herself – all twisted and contorted in an effort to keep warm. And there was so little feeling left in her body that she would have sworn her feet had dropped off, except for the fact that she could actually see them. The cold, previously unnoticed, was now descending upon her like an avalanche.

As quickly as her frozen fingers would allow, Lucy began to rip the covers off the beds.

"Wrap yourself up!" she shouted to Hugh. "Quickly!" For once the desperation in her voice persuaded Hugh to do as he was told.

"More!" cried Lucy. "As much as you can!" and she flung several of the covers across the floor. Now that she was aware of the urgency of the situation, Lucy was beginning to panic. A dreadful numbness seemed to seize her from inside, freezing her heart and pumping its icy flow around her body.

Over on the other side of the room Hugh stood, his shoulders hunched, the blankets hanging in tattered folds about his shivering frame. With a soft sigh, he slumped down on to the floor. Without the energy to fight the cold, Hugh now cowered beneath its onslaught.

"Get up, Hugh!" cried Lucy, tugging at his arm. "Get up! We've got to keep moving! We've got to get warm!"

But try as she might, Lucy couldn't pull him to his feet. It was as if he was weighted to the ground.

"Please, Hugh!" begged Lucy. She was shaking him so hard that his head was rolling round like a demented puppet. But Hugh was oblivious to what was happening. Lucy watched him slowly close his eyes.

"Wake up!" she yelled. "Wake up!" She took his hand and clasped it tight in desperation.

"I know!" she murmured, talking more to herself now than to Hugh. "We'll use each other!" There was a sharp cry, followed by a deep silence. Lucy bit her lip and carried on.

"People always do that when they're cold," she whispered. "They put their arms round each other and huddle together for warmth," and with that she moved to embrace her brother.

With the sudden impulse of one who has had an electric shock, Hugh shot into the air.

"NO!" he screamed, in a voice of abject terror. Lucy swung round, expecting to confront whatever new horror had befallen them. And it was only when she discovered that there was nothing there, that Lucy realized Hugh was talking to her.

"NO! GET OFF!" he was shrieking. "I don't care what's happened. You're not CUDDLING me!"

Lucy froze momentarily, unable to believe what she had heard. Meanwhile, Hugh was already backing off across the floor.

"Get away! You're not to touch me! I'd rather die of cold!"

Lucy fixed her brother with a look of utter disbelief and started to pursue him round the room.

"Don't be so ridiculous, Hugh," she yelled. "I was only going to rub your back!" and she pounced on him and dragged him to the ground, where Hugh started wrestling madly. Stronger though she was, Lucy couldn't get him into a position where she could pin him down. Hugh was fighting as if his very life depended on it. Whatever senses he could be described as possessing, it was as if they had suddenly come back to him. It was bad enough that he had been beguiled into holding Lucy's hand! But what would his friends at school say if they knew he had been rubbed and cuddled by a girl? For a split second the dual images of Beefy Keith and Spiky Isaacs flashed mockingly before Hugh's eyes. Of all the things that had happened to him that night, this was quite the most horrific so far.

At last Hugh managed to struggle free, while Lucy

collapsed in a gasping heap on the floor. And it wasn't until he had made completely sure that she had finished that Hugh, his honour still intact, collapsed as well. The fight had had one advantage – it had warmed them up, probably better than anything else.

Lucy lay flat on her back, panting and staring up at the ceiling. She was thinking over everything that had occurred: the nightmare, the transformation of the house, the mysterious barrier round the edge of the grounds, the rhythmic steps of the ghost-children. And still she couldn't work out what was more amazing – that, or this latest demonstration of her brother's extraordinary behaviour.

Chapter Five

As she lay in silent contemplation of the night's events, Lucy fell into a state of fitful half-sleep on the floor. Images tramped like soldiers through her mind, back and forth, round and round, searching for some meaning to the maze. It was as if she was reviewing everything through the eye of a camera: some things, like the ghost-children, loomed large and clear, as if magnified by the lens; others, like her mother, would appear from a great distance, blurred, as if slightly out of focus, then become gradually smaller and fade away. And throughout everything there was the rhythmic beat of marching feet, quiet at first, invading her sleep with the relentless insistence of a ticking clock, which grows louder with its constant repetition.

"Where do you want to go?" called Lucy in her dream. But the feet just kept on marching and pounding, endlessly searching for somewhere to stop. Then they turned and started moving towards

Lucy, nearer and nearer, louder and louder, deafening, pounding, sickening, pounding, threatening to trample her underfoot . . .

Lucy jolted bolt upright and opened her eyes. Immediately the hammering in her head died away and was replaced by the soft, steady sound of dripping water. She traced it to the basin in the corner of the room. The tap must have worked loose. Mesmerized, Lucy watched the slow formation of a tiny droplet, as it filled and distended like a miniature bulb, then with a faint splash trickled away. It stirred something deep within her memory: the clearness of the water, the ripple of its fall, the passing recollection of a nightmare, the sudden shudder of an unknown fear. But in an instant it was gone, dismissed, and Lucy turned off the tap and walked away.

"What shall we do now?" asked Hugh. It was his perpetual cry. Whenever he could think of nothing to do himself, Hugh would shift the responsibility for action to somebody else. Lucy watched her brother as he peeled off the blankets and flung them in an untidy mountain on the bed. He looked up at her expectantly, a mass of bony limbs and tousled hair with a great tuft that stuck up in the middle like a coconut. Lucy remembered how their mother was for ever trying to smooth it down.

"I don't know!" she snapped. Suddenly she was tired of being responsible, tired of making decisions, tired of having to act like an adult when she was only twelve years old. It wasn't so much that she minded looking after her brother. It was just that she wanted somebody to look after her. Lucy turned to the window and brushed away a tear. Where was her mother now?

Outside, the sun was rising in the winter sky,

casting a strange, unearthly glow over the marshland and staining the frozen surface of the lake with a blood-red tinge. Looking out, Lucy could fancy that she was on the very edges of the earth. All was still and deathly quiet, without even the strain of a bird song to herald the beginning of the day. Trees, stripped of their finery, reared like twisted witches from the snow, which covered the scene in a great white shroud. Nothing stood out to draw the attention. There were no peculiarities, no striking landmarks. The winter had endowed the landscape with a pale and uniform beauty, blinding the eyes and numbing the brain with a perfection which was tiresome to behold. Everything seemed somehow smooth, untouched, as if something beneath the surface had been glossed over.

Just as she was about to turn away, a sudden movement over to her right caught Lucy's eye. She glanced back to where a clump of charred brown bushes stretched their bony fingers to the sky. There it was again – a brilliant flash of colour, which seemed to dip and abruptly disappear, then reappear as it rose once more. It was a near-circular movement, the pattern of which was repeated over and over, and always the object would vanish about a metre above the ground. Other than that, it was impossible to say what it might be.

Lucy strained her eyes against the dazzling glare of the snow. For a moment she was blinded by its brilliance, then gradually she began to discern the faintest outline of a human form. A female form clad entirely in white so that it blended into the wintry backdrop. Only the hair stood out, a bright flame red, like a scorch mark. It was this that had first attracted Lucy's attention.

The woman, who was facing away from Lucy, seemed to be moving up and down, although it was too far for Lucy to work out exactly what she was doing. As Lucy watched, the oddest sensation started creeping through her body. Like a long fingernail, it tickled and scratched its way up her spine and across her back, tingling at the very tips of her fingers and prickling the roots of her hair. Lucy gave an involuntary shudder. Not for the first time that day, she recognized the first intimations of fear.

"Hugh!" she hissed. "Come here!" Hugh moved over to the window.

"Look," said Lucy, pointing towards the figure. "Over there." Hugh screwed up his eyes and followed the direction of Lucy's gaze.

"Well?" she muttered.

"Can't see anything," said Hugh.

"Look harder!"

"No. Nothing. Wait a minute! There is something. Something red. A red blob moving up and down!" declared Hugh triumphantly. "What is it?"

"Look again," said Lucy.

"I can't see anything else," said Hugh. "Hold on! Yes I can. It's a woman! A woman with bright red hair." Hugh turned to his sister. "What's she doing out there?"

"I don't know," said Lucy.

"Perhaps she can help us," cried Hugh excitedly. "Perhaps she can tell us where Mum is!"

"I don't think so," Lucy replied.

"Well I'm going to ask her!" announced Hugh, flinging the window wide open. The cold morning silence shattered like a myriad pieces of splintered glass.

"Hey!" he called. "We're up here! Over here!" Far

off, oblivious to Hugh's cry, the figure toiled end-lessly up and down, absorbed in some hidden task.

"Over here!" Hugh called again. "In the house." But still the woman didn't respond. She simply carried on, up and down, up and down, as relentless as the feet in Lucy's dream. Hugh glanced round, a puzzled frown on his forehead.

"She can't hear us, Hugh," whispered Lucy. Hugh stared at her blankly. Had he simply not understood? Or was he postponing the moment of recognition?

"She's like the children," said Lucy softly. "She's not real." Lucy watched as the memory of the children passed like a gentle wave across Hugh's face, to be instantly replaced by a swift tide of rising panic.

"Shut up!" he yelled. "Shut up! You're just saying that. You're just saying that to try and frighten me!" He was working himself into a frenzy.

"I'll prove it!" he was shrieking. "I'll prove to you that you're wrong!" And with that he started scream-ing hysterically out of the window.

Lucy covered her ears and closed her eyes. The sound pierced her like a dagger, tearing at her insides and opening her heart to the anguish which lay behind. It was as deliriously infectious as a fever, moving her to join in. And just as she was on the point of screaming too, Hugh suddenly stopped. Then came the shrill piping of his voice.

"I told you!" he was saying. "I told you she could hear us! I told you you were wrong!"

Lucy looked out across the snow to where the woman, now motionless, had turned and appeared to be staring towards the window. Then, as if startled, she moved swiftly back in the direction of the house.

Once again, the fingernail clawed and reawakened Lucy's fear.

"Look!" cried Hugh. "She's coming to see us! She's coming to help!"

As the woman came nearer, Lucy could see that she was wearing a long white coat that reached down to the ground and trailed out behind in horrible imitation of a wedding gown. Indeed, it gave the impression that she was actually walking on air, gliding fractionally above the surface of the snow. She was very tall and erect, with a corpse-like rigidity about her frame, although her movements were swift and smooth. Lucy could form no clear impression of her features, only a general pallor around her face, which was offset by the brilliance of her hair.

Now that she was closer, Lucy could tell that the woman was not, as she had originally thought, looking in their direction, but had her gaze intently fixed on some point further down. Lucy leaned far enough out of the window to enable her to see the corners of the house. She scanned the lower wings, then up and down the gabled front and through the dark mullioned windows. But she could see nothing unusual.

Finally her eyes came to rest on the two carved animal heads above the porch. They seemed to grimace and leer at her menacingly as if threatening to break free of the stare which held them prisoner. Lucy followed the line of the pillar down towards the ground, still searching for some sign of whatever was drawing the woman's attention. And then she saw them, caught in a sudden slant of sunlight – two tiny pairs of feet. The rest of the figures were cast in shadow, standing as they were within the recess of the porch. But Lucy didn't need to see them. She knew every curve of their doll-like features, every curl on their porcelain heads. The image of those fragile forms was for ever etched in Lucy's memory. Now she could just make out their outlines as, framed beneath the arch of the doorway, the ghost-children clutched each other's hands in a haunting picture of desolation and despair.

"What are you looking at?" asked Hugh, leaning out of the window to follow the direction of Lucy's gaze. Lucy waited for his response, some sound to indicate that Hugh had seen them too. But there was nothing. Hugh was past screaming now, past exclamations of surprise, past reacting to every unexpected twist of a nightmare's tale. For the first time in his life, Hugh could think of nothing whatever to say and the room was filled with his silence.

Outside, the ghostly spectres met and turned and pursued their path up to the house.

Chapter Six

"They're coming inside!" yelled Lucy and she raced over towards the door. For a moment, Hugh thought that she was trying to get out.

"Don't go!" he cried. "Don't leave me!" Lucy turned, then smiled at her brother.

"It's all right, Hugh. I was only checking that the door was locked."

Hugh blushed. He was ashamed: not only of this latest outburst, but of his entire conduct throughout the night. He wasn't used to showing his real feelings and whereas this actually endeared him to Lucy, Hugh thought that it just made him look weak. Try as he might, Hugh couldn't suppress the notion that Lucy, as a mere girl, had coped with the situation far better than he had. And once this thought had occurred, he couldn't get it out of his head. Hugh wasn't a nasty or malicious boy. But he was one of those boys with a rather over-developed sense of competition, and while he admired his sister, he was also jealous of the fact that she had succeeded where he had failed. He leaned back against the wall and tried to assume the "casual, slightly disdainful, with a touch of brilliance" expression that he usually reserved for school football matches.

"Well that won't do much good," he remarked scornfully. Then, almost despite himself, he added, "What shall we do now?" Lucy sighed and sat down on the edge of the bed.

"Wait, I suppose. What else?" She flung herself back on the bed. If only she could sleep and forget everything for a while. Then, maybe, when she awoke, the nightmare would have passed. She sighed a deep sigh of fatigue and snuggled down into the warm dark comfort of the pillows. They were as soft and as soothing as her mother's embrace.

As she rolled over, Lucy was startled back into reality by a pricking sensation in her side. She sat up and ran her hand over the top of the bed. It came to rest on a small, hard object about the size of a ten-pence piece. As she picked it up, a shaft of sunlight caught the surface in a brilliant flash of green. With a surge of pleasure, Lucy recognized her mother's favourite brooch.

"Look, Hugh! Look what I've found!" said Lucy, handing the brooch to her brother. "It was on the bed." Hugh took the brooch and held it close to his chest.

"How did it get there?" he asked.

"I don't know," said Lucy. "I don't remember."

"Perhaps it's a sign!" cried Hugh excitedly. "To let us know she's all right."

"Perhaps," Lucy quietly replied. She took the brooch and traced the tiny filigree pattern with her finger. It was as fine and as delicate as the veins which laced their way through her mother's cheeks. It brought back so many memories: Christmases, birthdays, all the special occasions when she was allowed to wear it. And other, sadder, times, when Lucy wore the brooch as a kind of comfort – a reminder of the warm summer evening when she had sat outside and listened to her father's tale of a long-ago trip to the seaside, a blue-print dress and sand as golden as her mother's hair, of ice creams the colour of rainbows, of magic sideshows and fortune-tellers' dreams, and of the buying of a brooch as a first declaration of her parents' love.

What had happened since that time to make her father leave? As if searching for an answer, Lucy looked into the dark depths of the emerald and recalled happy days spent playing on the grassy banks of the lake, where the willows gushed in great green fountains down to the water's edge. Like a dark cloud in a summer's sky, a shadow passed across her mind. Was it because the lake had frozen over? Or was it because the willows, divested of their leafy robes, were weeping for a time long past?

As if to punctuate her mood, the wind whipped up against the window pane and tried to scratch and claw its way into the room. Lucy listened fearfully as it roared in angry defiance, then, with a long, low moan, pursued its lonely route across the marsh. Then back once more to the still cold silence and the snow, which fell as quietly as an untold secret.

"Listen!" said Hugh suddenly. "Don't you hear anything?" There came to Lucy's ears the fleeting impression of somebody weeping.

"It's just the wind," she replied. "Playing tricks."

"No. There it is again!" cried Hugh. "Listen." Once more the anguished cry came like a whisper on the wind, too human now to be a mere trick of nature, but as distant and remote as an echo from another century. At first it seemed to be coming from outside, and all around, as if whatever was making the sound was encircling the house. But then it started closing in, becoming gradually louder and nearer, until Lucy was able to pinpoint it to somewhere within the house. It was high-pitched and full of despair. There was no mistaking it now. It was the sound of a child crying.

"It's below us!" said Hugh, his ear pressed to the floor. "We've got to go down." Lucy grabbed him by the arm.

"We can't do anything," she said. She sat back on the bed and held tight to her brother's arm. Beneath them the crying continued, as mournful and wretched as a funeral wake. Lucy looked at the door and thought fearfully of the world beyond. Something seemed to be pulling her irresistibly towards it. She tensed her body in a gesture of defiance and a sharp stab of pain shot through her hand. Clenched tight inside her fist, Lucy remembered the small silver brooch with an emerald the colour of a willow tree.

Next to Lucy, Hugh sat white and rigid, his body racked with the pain of each new sob as it built to its pitiful crescendo.

"You're right," said Lucy, moving over to the door. "We *have* got to go down," and while she reached for the handle with one hand, with the other she pressed the brooch quietly to her lips.

Chapter Seven

Lucy and Hugh had not yet seen the rest of the house in full daylight. Under the shadow of the dawn it was still possible to hope that, as the hours wore on, the twilight would lift like a morning mist, carrying with it the grey unfamiliar shapes which formed no part of their ordinary daytime world. At least before, there was the small comfort that everything belonged to that obscure part of the night in which all strange happenings traditionally occurred. But now the sun shone with a cruel brilliance upon each unknown object, as if to underline the fact that it existed. And somehow it was even more frightening to watch the persistence of a nightmare under the broad light of day. It was as if everything had been turned round, the unusual had suddenly become usual and now it was Lucy and Hugh's world which hovered beneath a twilight shade.

Lucy took a deep breath and stared straight ahead. Looking along the corridor now she could imagine that she was looking down a vast, draughty passage going back in time. In the blindness of the night, it had seemed that it was crowded with all manner of mysterious things. Now Lucy was surprised to discover that the only furniture consisted of two large wooden chests, which stood like coffins on the bare boarded floor. For the first time she noticed that there was no carpet, or indeed anything which gave even the slightest impression of warmth. The only other decoration was the huge sombre portraits which lined the walls – sentries who seemed to devour with hungry eyes every movement that Lucy made.

"Wouldn't fancy meeting her on a dark night," muttered Hugh. He was referring to a painting of a young woman with red hair who was holding what appeared to be a white cat in her lap. From where she stood, Lucy thought the woman looked rather beautiful. It wasn't until she got nearer that the bright blue eyes started to glitter with an icy malevolence and the smile took on the aspect of a cruel sneer. Not even the cat could soften the picture, ensnared as it was by the long, slender fingers which hooked around the animal's throat like the talons of a bird of prey.

Lucy hurried on down the cold grey corridor. Beneath them, the sobbing had stilled to a plaintive whine, which shook the very walls with the resonance of its sorrow. Lucy shivered and pulled her dressing gown tight around her.

"Come on," hissed Hugh, who was standing at the top of the stairs.

It was strange, thought Lucy, how her brother could switch from extreme stupidity to jealousy and now to a selfless concern for others. Like a human chameleon, Hugh was constantly revealing himself in

31

different colours. Personally he disliked showing any emotion, but now his only thought was for the torment which lay behind somebody else's tears. Lucy wondered what unexpected form her brother's behaviour had yet to take.

As they descended the stairs and Lucy was able to look down upon the hall, she again had the impression that time had somehow lapsed. Perhaps it was the old-style furniture and the dust, which had settled everywhere like grey flour shaken from a giant sieve, or the grandfather clock, either stopped or broken, which seemed to hold the hours in suspension. Or perhaps it was the stale, choking air and the atmosphere of silent neglect, which hung as heavy as the particles of dust. Over by the door, Lucy could see a stuffed animal in a glass case, caught in the act of killing its prey. There hovered over everything the dark countenance of doom.

Suddenly Lucy noticed that the sobbing had stopped. At the foot of the stairs, Hugh was poised ready for it to start again. But there was nothing. With no sound to follow, they were unsure where to go.

"It seemed as if it was coming from underneath the bedroom," said Hugh.

"Must be in the dining room then," replied Lucy and she moved off across the hall. Ahead of them the passageway loomed large and empty. Before venturing forward, Lucy waited for her brother to catch up.

Holding their breath, the children pushed open the door to the dining room and went inside. Everything was still and ominously silent. Together they began to search quietly around. Like the rest of the house, there wasn't much furniture, but what there was was spartan and bare and made no concession to either vanity or comfort. There was no ornamentation, no small adornments, none of the soft lines and contours which give off an impression of homeliness. Everything had a hard-edged, metallic quality, although the furniture was made mostly out of a heavy dark wood which absorbed and swallowed the light.

Just at that moment there was a sudden noise in the passageway outside. Hugh dived for cover behind a huge tomb-like chair. But Lucy, who was standing over to one side of the room, was caught out in the open. She looked frantically around. There was a desk in front of her, but there was no room to crouch underneath it and it was pushed back against the wall so there was no possibility of hiding behind.

In a state of panic, Lucy swung round at the same time as a ghastly white figure appeared in the doorway. Lucy clapped her hands to her mouth in an effort to stifle a scream. Not only was this the woman she had watched from the window, it was also the woman in the portrait upstairs. The only difference was the hair which, piled into a gory crown upon her head, was still bright red save for a single streak of white running in a scar across the middle, and the eyes, no longer confined to canvas, now directed their evil glare like a searchlight around the room: peering, probing, scouring every shadow for some sign of what they sought. Cold at first, but getting warmer with each new shift of their deadly gaze, the eyes looked on, hotter and hotter, blazing, searching until, with a fearful surge, Lucy felt them come to rest upon her own small, shivering frame.

Chapter Eight

Lucy froze in terror as the eyes seemed to bore their way into her soul. A faint stench, as of rotting flesh, filled her nostrils. Was it her imagination or was it coming from the skins of the dead animals which littered the woman's frame? The woman was clad entirely in white fur. Round her neck there hung the stole of a cat, its eyes red and gleaming and its mouth curled in a perpetual grimace.

Unable to move, Lucy looked on in helpless dread as the woman advanced towards her. The cat, which had hitherto hung limply around the woman's neck, now bounced higher with each approaching step, as if preparing to unwind and fly at Lucy through the air. And all the time the steel-blue eyes glittered like the ice beneath the sun and hypnotized Lucy with their vile glare.

It was all Lucy could do to cover her face with her hands. Even so she could still sense the presence of the woman, closing on her as a hunter closes on its prey. Suddenly a wave of blistering heat passed through her body. Lucy gasped and choked. It felt as if her lungs were going to explode. She clutched at her throat while the water streamed from her eyes, and sizzled down her cheeks. And just as she started to recover her breath, it came again – turning her blood to molten lava and her heart to a cauldron about to erupt.

So intense was the effect that for a moment Lucy lost consciousness. She began to sink lower and lower, away from the heat and down into the cold, dark depths of she knew not what. And all the while she was locked in a struggle against her own suffocation.

When Lucy came to, the tears were still pouring down her cheeks. It gave her the strangest impression that she was looking at everything under water. With a frightened cry, she sat up and rubbed her eyes. As her vision cleared, she caught a fleeting glimpse of a tall white figure disappearing through the doorway and into the corridor beyond.

"WOW!" cried Hugh, leaping up from behind the chair. "BRILLIANT!"

Lucy lay back down on the floor. Her head was still swimming from the encounter.

"That was brilliant, Lu!" Hugh cried again. He only ever called her "Lu" when he was impressed by something – as a sort of token of his esteem. "She just walked straight through one side, then straight back through the other!" He gave Lucy a hearty slap on the back.

"It was like watching a horror movie!" he added, by way of consolation.

Lucy, still in a state of shock, had propped herself up against the wall. "I thought she was coming after me," she murmured.

"No. She just picked up an envelope from the desk behind," said Hugh. "You know," he added thoughtfully, "all those things people say about ghosts – about their being evil and all that – and it turns out they can't even see or hear us! Still, it means we haven't got so much to worry about."

Lucy closed her eyes in an effort to stop the room spinning round. She felt a bit like she did after coming off the waltzers at the fairground – green and giddy and without a stomach.

"Hugh . . .," she began. "Did you recognize her?" Hugh nodded.

"It was the woman from the portrait," he answered. "I wonder who she is." Lucy shrugged and, leaning back against the wall, buried her face in her hands. She was starting to feel sick again.

"Don't cry," said Hugh gently.

"I wasn't," muttered Lucy. Hugh stiffened indignantly.

"Yes you were," he replied. "I heard you!"

Lucy lifted her head to refute him but before she could speak, a sound, coming from the wall directly behind her, rose up to stop the words. Hugh turned, his eyes aflame with the sudden recognition. The childish sobbing had resumed its wretched lament.

"It's next door!" he cried, rushing across the room towards the corridor. Lucy staggered after him, as unsteady as a toddler on her feet.

"Wait!" she shouted. "The woman – she might still be there." But Hugh had already disappeared.

"It doesn't matter," she heard him yell back. "She can't see us anyway." Even so, Lucy checked the corridor before venturing out. She wasn't about to risk another encounter.

By the time Lucy reached the door, Hugh had

already opened it and was standing just inside. At first, she couldn't see the two tiny phantoms, obscured as they were by the huge oak table which stood like a monument in the centre of the room. They were seated just behind it on the floor, in front of the great stone fireplace. The boy was rocking backwards and forwards, sobbing bitterly; the girl was kneeling opposite, clutching his hands in hers. There was something almost brittle about their frames which, had they been real, suggested they would break upon the merest touch. Watching them now, Lucy felt her body begin to ache with a sorrow that she had never before known.

"Why is he crying?" asked Hugh, his voice tight with emotion. Just at that moment, the sobbing increased to a fevered pitch and the boy started tearing at his gown as wildly as if the thing was on fire. At the same time the girl rose to her feet and, taking hold of the garment at the neck, pulled it down over his shoulders. Lucy gasped in horror. Deep lashmarks striped their way across his back.

"Who did that?" screamed Hugh, his face white with anger. But the boy just kept on rocking, backwards and forwards, backwards and forwards, oblivious to Hugh's cry. While the girl, holding her brother's hands once more in hers, seemed to mirror every movement that he made. Fragile though they were, there was something rather unnerving about their likeness and in the way they seemed to move with one accord. Over everything they did there hung an air of silent communication, as if they intuitively understood each other's needs.

Now that the boy's clothing was no longer touching his wounds, his sobbing had eased with his pain. Hugh turned to his sister, quieter now as he fought back the tears which he was still ashamed to shed.

"Who would do a thing like that, Lucy?"

"I don't know," replied Lucy, adding incisively, "someone without a heart."

As if to underline what she had said, a voice cut like a whiplash through the air. It was a discordant, rasping sound, and so sharp and piercing that it grated on the nerves like broken glass. Immediately the sobbing stopped completely and the twins cowered in pitiful terror on the floor.

"Edward! Emily!"

Like animals to a slaughterhouse, the fragile spirits rose to meet their fate.

Chapter Nine

"Stop them!" cried Hugh as, ignorant of her presence, the tiny doll-like figures passed Lucy and moved swiftly on into the corridor beyond.

"How?" blurted Lucy. "They can't hear us! They can't see us! We can't even touch them! So how am I supposed to stop them from doing what they want?"

Hugh glared at his sister in frustration and then turned hurriedly away. Both of them were struck by the utter helplessness of their predicament. They couldn't get back to their own world, neither could they escape from the partial shadowy world in which their existence seemed to have no point. Suddenly they needed to find some reason, some purpose, some explanation for what had happened and why they were there.

"Come, on," said Lucy gently. "We need to sit down and think." She flung herself into a large wooden chair with a high panel at the back which curved over her head like a gravestone. Hugh followed suit. They stared at each other across the table. It was so tall that they were barely able to rest their elbows on its edge. Lucy tried desperately to formulate her thoughts. She was so confused that she wasn't even sure exactly what it was that was confusing her. And her nerves were as tattered as if they had been put through a shredding machine. At last, it was Hugh who began to speak.

"What bothers me," he said slowly, "is that we're getting all worked up about two children who are ghosts." He hesitated for a second, then went on.

"What I mean is . . . if they're dead . . . then presumably nothing more can happen to them."

"Then how come they're so frightened?" asked Lucy. "And so sad? Even if they are ghosts, their feelings are real enough."

"All right," said Hugh. "But as you said, what can we do about it?"

"What I can't understand," began Lucy, "is why the woman was so hot. When she walked through me, that is. I thought ghosts were supposed to be cold."

"And those cuts on the boy's back!" added Hugh. "I never would have thought a ghost could bleed." He paused momentarily.

"They just seem so real," he went on. "I mean, I know we can't touch them or anything. But somehow it's hard to believe they're dead."

The words jarred in Lucy's mind. Suddenly she was struck by an idea. It was like coming to the end of a long dark tunnel.

"Perhaps they're not!" she cried. Hugh looked at her questioningly.

"Perhaps they're not dead!"

"But how . . .?" began Hugh.

"Look around you!" interrupted Lucy. "Go on.

Look! What does it remind you of?"

"I don't know," faltered Hugh. "It's a bit like being in a museum."

"Exactly!" shrieked Lucy in excitement. "And what does a museum remind you of?" Hugh thought for a moment, then gave up.

"I don't know!" he snapped.

"Come on!" shouted Lucy. "It's important." She glared at her brother impatiently. "Think!" she yelled.

"Well," he answered, "I suppose it reminds me of the past." Lucy clapped her hands in delight.

"Exactly!" she cried again. Hugh shrugged his shoulders in irritation.

"So?" he said sarcastically. He felt a bit as he did when he was the last person to guess the answer to a game.

"Don't you see?" said Lucy. "In a way we are in a museum. Because somehow we've been transported back into the past!"

Hugh stared at his sister in jealous disbelief. Lucy's idea was such a good one that he couldn't bear the fact that it wasn't his own. He tried to give vent to one of his biggest and best guffaws. It came out more like a burp.

"No. Listen!" urged Lucy. "It all makes sense. You know what you were saying about the children seeming real? About their not being ghosts?" Hugh nodded grudgingly.

"Well they are real! They're alive – but in their own time."

"So how come they can't see or hear us?" asked Hugh, bent on defeating Lucy's theory.

"Because we don't exist in their time," she replied. "But we can see and hear them because, in a sense,

41

they have already happened.'

"Well in that case we should be able to touch them as well!" announced Hugh triumphantly. For a moment it seemed that he had Lucy on the run. As if in a game of snakes and ladders, she stood poised at the head of the snake. Then in one swift movement, she passed on to the foot of the ladder.

"No," she answered, steadily climbing each rung. "We wouldn't be able to touch them because in our time they wouldn't exist. They would have died years before."

"But what about all the furniture?" persisted Hugh. Now it was his turn to flounder. "We can touch that."

"Yes, because it's quite possible that all this furniture still exists somewhere in our own time." With an imperceptible WHOOSH! Hugh slid down to the bottom of the snake.

"So how far, in your expert opinion, have we gone back in time?" he asked, trying to inject a note of scorn.

"I'm not sure," said Lucy. "The furniture and their clothes are so plain it's difficult to tell. About one hundred years, I should think. Maybe less. Maybe more."

"And what about our bedroom?" cried Hugh, as if he had thrown a six. "How do you explain the fact that everything in the house has changed except that?" There was a long silence while Lucy mulled the question over in her mind.

"I think partly because we were in it at the time," she answered slowly. "I also think it has to be the key to our escape. That and . . ." she stopped abruptly, as if distracted. The dice lay unthrown on the board.

"And what?" asked Hugh, pressing home his advantage.

"The lake . . .," she murmured fitfully. "Something to do with the lake . . ." Hugh stared at his sister in bewilderment.

"The lake?" he remarked scathingly. Now she wasn't making any sense at all.

Lucy struggled to recall some fact deep down in the mine of her memory, while her thoughts whirled in dark confusion and an unknown terror took possession of her soul. As the seconds ticked by, a sudden shaft of sunlight shot through the window, trapping thousands of particles of dust in its beam. Lucy gazed at them, tiny specks of phosphorescence in a lurid prison. Somewhere, deep inside her consciousness, it reminded her of her own condition. She followed the stream of light down to the floor, where it seemed to collect in a pool of brilliance upon the exact spot that the twins had recently occupied – except in the centre, where the brightness was diffused by a dull dark object absorbing the light. Automatically, Lucy narrowed her eyes in an effort to discern what the object was. She bent down to pick it up. It was an old black-and-white photograph enclosed in a battered leather frame.

"Look," said Lucy, holding up a trembling hand. "It was on the floor. Where the children were."

The photograph was of a young man and woman, taken from the shoulders up. The woman, who was facing straight out, had her head slightly inclined towards the man, who seemed to be whispering something in her ear. Both of them were laughing.

There was such a strong sense of intimacy about the pair that even by looking at the photograph Lucy had the impression that she was somehow intruding on their privacy. She gazed awkwardly at the faces. The man was of a darker complexion, his hair fairer, although it was difficult to get any real sense of colour, and he had a broad frame which suggested he was tall. His features were large and gentle, with nothing particularly remarkable about them, save perhaps for the eyes which were unusually light and piercing. It was the woman who really drew the children's attention. She had the timeless beauty of a statue about her features, which were so fine and delicate they could have been chiselled out of marble: the exquisite curve of her cheek, the wide haunting eyes, the hair which fell in thick curls around her shoulders and the tiny hand which brushed it from her brow. And yet there was nothing cold about her appearance. She looked so happy, so radiant, there was so much fun in that unknown face, that Lucy felt a sudden rush of warmth.

"Are you thinking what I'm thinking?" asked Hugh.

"That she's the children's mother?" Hugh nodded. The similarity was too striking to be dismissed.

"So that could be their father," added Lucy. "Although there's something else about him . . . I'm not sure what."

Hugh, who had been fiddling with the photograph, accidentally detached it from its case. It fell on to the floor.

"Hey. Look!" he cried, picking it up. "There's some writing on the back." He tried to decipher the spidery hand. The ink had blotted in several places.

"Margaret and David . . ." he read out slowly. "A-l-b . . . I can't make out the surname."

"Let me see," said Lucy. Hugh reluctantly handed her the photograph. She gazed at it for several seconds.

44

"I don't know," she muttered. "Elliot? Abbot?" The name seemed to strike a chord. "Abbot . . . Abbot . . ." she repeated over to herself. "Of course!" she cried, with a vehemence that made Hugh jump. "John Abbotson!"

Hugh looked at his sister with obvious annoyance. All these stupid guessing games! Why couldn't she just come to the point? As if reading her brother's thoughts, Lucy started to explain.

"John Abbotson was the man who first built and owned this house!"

"So what?" said Hugh, attempting to cover with his sarcasm the fact that he had failed to grasp the significance of her statement.

"Well, if the people in the photograph are called Abbot then they could be related to John Abbotson – names often change a bit over the years . . ."

"And?" prompted Hugh.

"And if they are his descendants," continued Lucy, "then it's quite likely that they would carry on living in his house. Which more or less proves my theory: that we've gone back in time and the people we are seeing are the people who used to live in this house!"

"But we haven't seen those people!" said Hugh.

"No, but we've seen their children," replied Lucy.

"Well if the woman in the photograph is the children's mother, then who's that horror with the red hair?"

"I don't know!" snapped Lucy. "I can't answer every question at once."

"Besides," Hugh went on, "how do you know who used to own the house?"

"Because I've read the inscription on the porch," she answered. "It says: 'built in 1590 by John

45

Abbotson for himself'. Haven't you read it?" Hugh reddened. The only inscriptions he ever read were the ones in the toilets at school. He sank down in his chair and heaved a deep sigh of defeat. Back on the snakes and ladders board, Lucy was nearing the home square.

"All right," he conceded. "Supposing you are right and we *have* gone back in time. We still haven't worked out *why* we're here."

"To help the children, I suppose," said Lucy. "Although we don't seem to be able to do anything. Besides, we don't even know what's wrong." Hugh brightened perceptibly. Suddenly he could see a role for himself. What did it matter if he didn't have as many ideas? Thinking was girl's stuff! And Hugh was a man of action!

"Then I suggest we go and find out!" he declared, pushing the chair vigorously away. And with that he strode purposefully off towards the door.

Chapter Ten

Replacing the photograph so the children could find it, Lucy followed Hugh out of the room. She had no idea how long they had been in there, but by the way the shadows had shortened she guessed it must be getting on towards midday. Outside in the corridor it was impossible to tell. There were no windows and the resulting gloom had a timeless quality about it, as if untouched by the hours which passed it by. Everything which stood there seemed somehow ageless, dateless, caught in a dreary state of limbo. Lucy could imagine that it was the kind of place in which she might never grow old.

She hurried on through the gloom. It was hard to believe that this was the same house in which she lived. It had always been dark in places, but before darkness had been fresh and exciting; now it was stifling and oppressive and seemed to wring the oxygen from the air. Even moving from the corridor into the lightness of the hall brought little relief.

Wherever she went, Lucy found it difficult to breathe.

Lucy closed her eyes in an effort to remember how their own hall looked. Immediately the grandfather clock was replaced by a table piled high with directories and a telephone by its side. The bare stone floor was covered by a faded patterned rug, with the faintest trace of a coffee stain in the corner from where their mother had tripped over Hugh's skate-board. And in the place of the macabre stuffed animal there hung a painting, although Lucy struggled to remember what it was of. She was just about to ask, when Hugh spoke first:

"Why aren't there any servants around?" he demanded. "Wouldn't they have had servants a hundred years ago?"

It was a question which had been bothering Lucy too. The house was so big. She remembered the first time she had ever seen it: the crumbling walls, the overgrown garden and the lake, a great blue looking-glass which reflected every season as it passed. Even deserted and derelict, the house had seemed so full of possibilities. Of course it was only because it was in such disrepair that they had been able to afford it. Lucy recalled her parents' excitement and the air, which was charged with plans and opportunities. By the time their father had left, the house was only half complete. From then on, their mother had worked on it herself. It was like repairing a broken promise.

"I don't know," Lucy replied, in answer to Hugh's question. "Perhaps we just haven't seen them yet."

"Come to that," Hugh went on. "Where are the children?" The house seemed strangely deserted.

"Let's try down there," said Lucy, indicating the passageway on the opposite side of the hall. They had only ever used that part of the house for storage, or for the occasional game of hide-and-seek. Never for living in – mainly because it wasn't finished. Besides, Lucy remembered her mother saying, "Any more rooms and the three of us will be rattling round this place like peas in a drum". Strange, thought Lucy, how the absence of one person could make everything seem so empty.

Hugh strode off in the direction that Lucy was pointing.

"Follow me!" he cried, his face set in a mask of grim determination. Like an ancient warrior, he clenched his hands in fists of iron and marched resolutely on across the hall. He marvelled at his own courage and dismissed any thoughts that it was due to the fact that he knew he couldn't be seen or heard. For Hugh, the whole encounter was becoming something of a glorious adventure, to be recounted in every gory detail for the wonder of his friends at school. He closed his eyes and his head filled with gasps of admiration and imaginary applause. The awestruck faces of Beefy Keith and Spiky Isaacs floated once more into his mind. Never again would he shrink before their gaze!

"This way!" he cried again, sallying forth with an ever increasing vigour. For the first time since Hugh had fallen over in the corridor upstairs, Lucy wanted to giggle.

The passageway was the same as she remembered it: very bare and tinged with the musty smell of disuse. Only the walls were significantly different, as if they had been recently whitewashed, adding an incongruous touch of brilliance to the otherwise dismal surround. The first door they came to was locked. Hugh tugged forcefully at the handle, encouraged in his bravery by the fact that he knew he couldn't get in. He moved purposefully on, applying the same amount of pressure to the next door, which he was confident would also be locked. But it swung easily open and with a surprised cry Hugh fell into the room. Lucy arrived just in time to see the three figures who were already inside turn simultaneously to face the door.

For a few agonizing moments, Lucy thought they had made a terrible mistake. The woman was staring straight at her: she could see see Lucy after all! It was like a recurring nightmare. Mesmerized, Lucy watched the figure advance towards her and felt her skin begin to tingle with the woman's approach. It was a curious mixture of sensations, like fire and ice, and both so intense as to be almost identical, so that in the end Lucy couldn't tell whether she was gasping from the heat or from the cold.

Just as the woman was almost upon her, Hugh scrambled to his feet and flung Lucy back against the wall. Immediately the woman paused, her body taut with a sense that she had never before known: some faint sound as if from nowhere, a slight disturbance of the air, the vague feeling that all was not quite as it should be. Then, with a dismissive laugh, she turned and slammed the door shut.

The woman walked back to where the twins stood, mute and trembling, holding each other's hands. Her footsteps rang hollow on the grey stone floor and her skirt rustled like the wind amongst dead leaves. A long cane twitched and quivered in her grasp.

"We might have known it was her who was beating them!" whispered Hugh savagely.

"Shhh!" said Lucy. For the woman had started to speak.

"We'll say no more about it," she began. "I think you've learnt your lesson." The twins stared up at her, silent and afraid.

"Well?" she continued. "Edward?"

"Yes, Aunt."

"Emily?"

"Yes, Aunt."

"Well? What do you say?"

"Thank you, Aunt," murmured the children.

"What?" rasped the woman. "I can't hear you!"

"Thank you, Aunt!" said the children again.

Barely able to contain himself, Hugh struggled to break free of Lucy's hold.

"She's a monster!" he yelled.

"We can't do anything!" cried Lucy. "Not until we've found out what's happening. Now listen!"

The woman's voice grated and crackled like a scratched record. "I suppose you thought you'd have a fine old time," she was saying. "Living with Aunty and getting up to all your nasty tricks." She tickled the boy under the chin with the tip of her cane. "Isn't that right?"

"Y-yes, Aunt," he replied.

"Well you were wrong," she went on. "Your parents were far too soft with you. I'm in charge now!" and she began to flick the end of the cane against the palm of her hand. Then suddenly, she seemed to change her tack.

"Of course," she added in a more wheedling tone. "You know I'm only strict because I want the best for you." She rounded on the little girl like a hungry wolf.

"You do know that, don't you, dear?" Emily nodded a frightened reply.

"I don't want you to think that I don't care about

51

you. I don't want you to do anything silly like . . . running away." Her voice was the honeyed voice of a viper. "After all, Daddy wouldn't have wanted me to look after you if he'd thought I didn't love you. I am his sister, you know!"

The words went round and round in Lucy's head. Of course! The man in the photograph! She knew there was something else about him – something she couldn't quite explain. His features were so large and gentle, so different in every way, except for the eyes, which had the same strange, piercing light. She might have guessed from looking at them that this woman was his sister.

The woman stood up abruptly, as if satisfied that she had made her point.

"Off you go then," she commanded, waving her hand dismissively. The children started towards the door.

"And remember what I said," she hissed after them. "You're not to go outside without first asking my permission." The woman turned to look out of the window.

"You know what will happen if you do."

Immediately the children stopped and began to shift uneasily on their feet. Over by the window they could hear the steady tapping of the cane against the frame. Once more the woman seemed to check herself and, tucking the cane under her arm, she broke into a sudden smile. Lucy had never seen anything look so unnatural. Beware the smile of the crocodile, she thought quietly to herself.

"After all," added the woman, in a velvety tone, "we don't want you catching cold!" She paused momentarily, as if to monitor the effect of her words. She tried to laugh, but the laugh choked and spluttered in her throat and died before it was born. Finally she signalled impatiently for the children to leave.

"Well, go on!" she snapped. "What are you waiting for?" And the children turned and hurried towards the door.

Chapter Eleven

As a little girl, Lucy had always longed to be invisible. It was her most cherished dream. Whenever she read a story in which somebody was granted a wish, she would think to herself: if that was me, I would wish that I could have as many wishes as I liked for the rest of my life. And if that wasn't allowed, I would wish that I was invisible. Then she would make a list in her head of all the things she would be able to do: like stay up late and watch the television, or disappear when they had cauliflower cheese for tea. But as the realms of possibility diminished with her growing years, Lucy's desire gradually faded and the world became a rather more ordinary place.

At least until early that morning, when Lucy's own world had vanished along with everything else that was normal and her long-forgotten dream had been fulfilled. Being invisible now was nothing like Lucy had imagined it all those years before. Then she had envisaged that it would be a state which she could slip in and out of at will. Now it had a horrible air of permanency about it so that it lost all its sense of excitement. And the longer it went on, the more Lucy had the creeping sensation that she might indeed be disappearing. In fact, without Hugh to vouch for the fact that she was there, she might even have begun to wonder whether she existed at all.

And of course there was the added frustration that she couldn't be heard. She had never really considered that before. But having been flung into a situation which seemed to require her to act, she found that she was powerless to do anything at all. Lucy sighed a deep sigh of despair. Having once longed for the impossible, now all she wanted was for things to be normal once more.

She watched despondently as, oblivious to her presence, the twins moved hurriedly past and on towards the door. A warmth, as gentle as a summer breeze, lingered momentarily in the air. Then once again the fear swept like a tornado through the room and seemed to hover just above those tiny forms. An unwilling spectator, Lucy looked on as, hastened by their terror, the children fumbled for the handle on the door. Their frailty served only to underline her utter helplessness.

"STOP!" cried a voice, as venomous as the sting in a scorpion's tail. Lucy glanced round to see the woman, no longer by the window, gliding across the room to where the twins stood poised, one hand upon the other, ready to turn the handle of the door. The woman's shawl, which hung in two great jowls from her shoulders, billowed out behind like a parachute as she swooped upon the children. For one sickening second, Lucy thought she was going to strike them. But suddenly she stopped and bending down picked something bright and shimmering off the grey stone floor. As if from nowhere, the fleeting image of a willow tree flashed through Lucy's mind. Something was wrong . . . something was missing . . .

"What's this?" shrieked the woman, holding the object aloft. With a gasp of dismay, Lucy recognized her mother's brooch.

"How did she get that?" whispered Hugh.

"I don't know," Lucy replied. "I must have dropped it."

Too afraid to turn round, the twins stood, still facing the door, as the woman closed in upon them. Her body, contorted with rage, writhed and twisted in the manner of a serpent preparing to strike.

"What's this?" she screamed again, turning the twins like corkscrews with the force of her voice. Lucy looked at the brooch in the woman's hand. It seemed to have lost some of its lustre, as if the emerald had misted over.

"We-we don't know," stammered the children. The cane arched cat-like in the woman's grasp.

"I told you before," she hissed. "Anything like this you must give to me!" The children trembled and made no reply. The woman unleashed the tip of her cane. It seemed to fizz and cut back through the air. Then once again the velvety tone coated her voice like honey on sandpaper.

"I only want to keep everything safe," she cooed. "Things like this could be very valuable. You wouldn't want them lost! You wouldn't want to grow up and find everything had gone!"

Over by the wall, Hugh was fit to burst.

"Keep them safe!" he exploded. "You don't want to keep them safe. You just want to keep them for yourself!" Lucy was having the utmost difficulty restraining him.

"You socking great bag!" he yelled at the woman. The insult fell upon deaf ears. Hugh turned to his sister, purple with frustration.

"Why can't we do anything?" he screamed. Lucy paused, hoping that the silence might calm him down.

"I think we can," she replied. "We just have to find the way." Hugh folded his arms and slid down the wall to the floor. Some adventure this was turning out to be! He thought of all his heroes: Spiderman, He-man, James Bond. They didn't have to sit back and do all this girlie listening!

Meanwhile the woman was fawning over the children with the artful affection of a cat who wants its dinner.

"Now, my dears," she purred, "tell me where you got this brooch." The twins stared blankly at the unknown object and said nothing. Lucy watched the artificial smile twist and threaten to collapse.

"No need to be frightened, my dears," whined the woman, patting the children on their heads. They shrank before the contact. "I shan't be cross if you tell me the truth. Now, have you any more little trinklets like this?" She waited eagerly for their answer, but for the second time the twins made no reply. Once again, Lucy got the haunting impression that they were speaking to each other through the silence. The woman too was unnerved.

"Stop it!" she hissed, turning in an instant from kitten to spitting cougar. "I know what you're doing!" She lifted the cane high into the air where it hung like a wand about to strike its ruin on the world. Instinctively, Lucy ducked down and covered her face with her hands. A wave of nausea swept over her and her head began to whirl with the ferocity of a spinning top.

"NO!" cried Hugh, the sound issuing from his throat with the vehemence of a sob. The woman stood for a moment, one arm raised, a ghastly living sculpture. Then she slowly lowered the cane.

"No . . ." she said, a mocking echo of Hugh's cry. "This time we'll try a different way." The woman paused as, inexplicably and with one accord, all four children in the room looked up and awaited her explanation.

"You don't like the dark, do you, my dears?" the woman began. The twins stared mutely across, unsure how best to react. Lucy thought she could detect a slight quiver on the little boy's lip.

"Imagine a forest in the dead of night: the howling of unseen creatures, the gleaming of unknown eyes, the beating of wings behind you and the fear of danger ahead. Frightening, isn't it?" sneered the woman.

"You don't know where you are. You can't see where you're going. But at least you can run. Yes. It's a very big forest. There's lots of space. At least you can try to escape."

A sound, like the soft cry of a puppy, passed almost imperceptibly round the room. The woman's lips curled with malicious pleasure. She spun her evil web of intrigue and waited, spider-like, for her victims to be caught. She wove on and sensed power in the palm of her hand.

"What could possibly be worse than all that? Unless . . ." she paused and moved nearer to the children. "Unless . . . suddenly . . . there was nowhere else to run . . . everything began closing in upon you . . . Imagine, in the pitch black of night, all that was dark and unknown, all that fear – and you, in a space so small, unable to escape!" With a snarl, the woman pounced on the twins and hauled them by their gowns into the air.

"Now get in there!" she screamed and, opening the door of a small cupboard set back into the corner of the wall, she hurled the children inside. There rang out a final desperate cry, resonating through the room and down the walls into the foundations of the house, until the very fabric vibrated to its sorrowful tune. So wretched was the sound, so full of torment, that it seemed to span vast generations. It was like a cry from the beginning of time.

With a smile, the woman closed the door, turned the key, and walked away.

Chapter Twelve

As soon as the woman was out of the room, Hugh staggered over to the cupboard and started to tug feverishly at the handle. But the door remained firmly locked.

With a faint moan, he sunk to the floor. His misery sapped his strength and his weakness brought on a kind of dark delirium. As the flame of hope fluttered and died within him, it was replaced by the dull ache of resignation and Hugh stared defeat in the face.

For a moment, Hugh thought he was outside. The snow fell around and above him, endless and silent, covering his body in an icy down. The coldness numbed his pain. It was empty, soothing, without feeling. Hugh snuggled deep into oblivion.

"Hugh! Hugh!" He opened his eyes.

"You can't go to sleep now!"

"So . . . cold," muttered Hugh.

"What?" said Lucy. "Wake up! We've got to help them."

"Help – who?" murmured Hugh.

"The twins!" cried Lucy in exasperation. "Edward and Emily!" The names spun round in a whirlpool of confusion. Mere words at first, without shape – until gradually they began to take form and blurred figures became pale faces, with features as fine as gossamer and fear imprinted upon each one. Hugh sat up and rubbed his eyes. Some of the cold seemed to leave him as a flame rekindled within.

"Where are they?" he asked in a daze.

"In there!" replied Lucy, pointing impatiently at the cupboard. "What's wrong with you?"

"I don't know. Nothing," said Hugh quietly. "I must have been dreaming." Lucy stared at her brother uncertainly, then turned away.

"If only I hadn't dropped the brooch," she sighed, the guilt rising in a tide from her stomach. She looked around the room. It was stark and bare. There was nothing of any use.

"Have you got anything to pick the lock?" Hugh felt in his pyjama pocket and pulled out a free gift from a cereal packet and a piece of rock-hard chewing gum.

"No," he answered. He turned the chewing gum over in his hand. It was as solid as a stone. It must have been there for ages.

"Lucy," he began inquisitively. "Do you feel hungry at all?" Lucy looked up from searching the floor.

"No," she said. "Not really."

"Odd, isn't it?" remarked Hugh.

"Very odd," said Lucy smirking. "Considering how much you normally eat." Unusually, Hugh didn't rise to the challenge.

"I wonder if the time-scale is different," he mused.

Lucy regarded her brother in amazement.

"What do you know about time-scales?" she asked.

"Mrs Picton talked to me about it in class," Hugh went on. "When I was reading 'The Lion, the Witch and the Wardrobe' by C.S. Lewis." Lucy gasped incredulously and tried to remember if Aslan had ever played football.

"You mean you actually read it?" Hugh nodded.

"All of it?"

"Yes," replied Hugh casually. "And no matter how long the children spent in Narnia, it took up hardly any time at all in their own world."

"So?" said Lucy, resuming her search for something to pick the lock.

"Well, if it's the same as here, it could explain why we're not hungry," concluded Hugh. Lucy stopped in surprise. It wasn't often her brother made an intelligent remark.

"I suppose it could," she replied with sudden interest. "So when we get back to our own time . . ." She paused. She had nearly said "if".

". . . It could be that in between us going and returning nothing will have happened at all. I wonder if we'll even remember anything." Hugh looked alarmed and thought of all the lost opportunities for the adulation of his friends at school.

"Of course we'll remember!" he snapped.

"Here we are!" cried Lucy, picking a thin piece of metal off the floor. It looked like a pin from one of the door hinges. "We can use this." She moved back to the cupboard. There was not a sound, not a whisper. Lucy imagined the terror behind the door: the eyes, liquid with anticipation, shining in the dark and the silence screaming with untold fears.

"How could she?" Lucy murmured, not realizing she was speaking out loud.

"How could anyone?" came Hugh's reply.

Lucy inserted the pin into the lock and started to twist it round.

"Where do you think their parents are?" asked Hugh.

"Gone away maybe," said Lucy. "Or . . ."

"Or what?" prompted Hugh. There was a pause.

"Who knows?" Lucy replied, renewing her struggle with the lock.

"I wonder why she hates them so much," continued Hugh.

"Who?" muttered Lucy, concentrating her attention on the door.

"The woman. The Dread Aunt!" responded Hugh. "Perhaps she just hates everybody!"

"No. I think there's more to it than that." Lucy sat up and handed Hugh the pin. "Here. You have a go."

Hugh settled down and with one eye closed tried to focus his attention on the job in hand. He used to be ace at picking locks in his double agent phase. There was a definite knack to it . . . a certain twist of the fingers . . . a sharp flick of the wrist . . . With a soft clink, the pin fell from Hugh's hand and rolled off across the floor. He watched it despondently.

"It's no good," said Lucy. "We'll have to try and get the key back somehow."

"What? From the Dread Aunt!" spluttered Hugh.

"Well at least she can't see us," replied Lucy. "And anyway, I want to get Mum's brooch. She's not keeping that."

"I miss Mum," said Hugh unexpectedly.

"Yes," said Lucy softly. "So do I."

Chapter Thirteen

Lucy and Hugh retraced their steps out of the room and back into the hall.

"Where to now?" asked Hugh.

As if searching for an answer, Lucy looked around. Behind them and in front the corridors yawned dark and dank, fissures in the smooth pale surface of the walls. To their left the staircase, already half in shadow, rose to an even gloomier reception in the corridor above. While to their right the heavy oak door seemed to stretch out its handle in a mocking gesture of assistance and offered no retreat. Ahead of them, the grandfather clock stood pressed like an intruder against the wall and silently surveyed the scene. Its hands had stopped just short of twelve o'clock. Was that noon or midnight, Lucy wondered. What did it mean? Were they doomed to an endless morning without rest? Or an endless day in which a new dawn never broke? Was time at a standstill here?

Lucy rushed to the front door and flung it open

wide. The freezing air bit into her flesh and cleared her head. Outside the sun climbed high above a marble landscape, which shimmered and glittered beneath its gaze. It was a sure indication that time was on the move.

Lucy heaved a sigh of relief. As long as the hours ticked by, she felt that it brought nearer the point of their release.

"Sh-shut the door," shivered Hugh. His voice shook Lucy from her reverie.

"It's hard enough to get warm in this place as it is." She slammed the door to.

"What were you doing anyway?"

The question caught Lucy off guard. She didn't want to have to explain. Some things were best left unsaid. She crossed her fingers in anticipation of the lie.

"I . . . I was looking to see if the Dread Aunt was outside . . ."

"Well?" persisted Hugh.

"She wasn't," answered Lucy hurriedly. She sought for something to cover her confusion. "We'll have to search inside the house," she said.

"OK," agreed Hugh, grateful for the suggestion. At that moment a ray of sunlight glancing off the glass case near the door attracted Lucy's attention. The stuffed animal glinted wickedly at her from inside. The sight of it jogged Lucy's memory.

"Hugh," she began. "That picture . . . the one that used to hang over there . . ." She indicated the blank spot on the wall behind the case. "What was it of?" Hugh shrugged his shoulders carelessly.

"Dunno," he said with disinterest. Lucy tutted an impatient rebuke.

"So where shall we start?" asked Hugh. She

looked at him questioningly.

"Searching the house!" he added, by way of an explanation.

"Oh!" replied Lucy. "Well – I suppose that's as good a place as any," and she pointed to the corridor on the opposite side of the hall.

It did not take them long to find the Dread Aunt. As they retraced their steps back to the dining room, they discovered that the door had been left half open and through the gap they could just make out her figure slumped over the desk on the far side of the room.

Immediately Lucy thought something dreadful had happened. She clapped her hands to her mouth in an effort to stifle her dismay. Then, as the initial shock subsided, she became aware of a low growling sound, like a death rattle, quiet at first, but gradually gaining in its intensity and menace.

"What is it?" she trembled. "That noise. Like a wild beast. A monster. It's horrible!" She looked to her brother for some sort of consolation. But Hugh's face was bright red and as crinkled as a piece of old parchment. He was getting hysterical again.

Suddenly a loud peal of laughter filled the air. Lucy stiffened, hardly able to believe her ears. It was so unexpected, so out of place – like a breath of spring on a winter's day, a bubbling gurgling brook before the freeze. Lucy felt her mouth begin to twitch and quiver irresistibly. Beside her, Hugh was bent nearly double, his arms clasped agonizingly about his stomach, his face dripping with the flow of uninterrupted tears. His whole body was racked with the delicious pain of helpless laughter.

"What is it?" sniggered Lucy. "What are you laughing for?" Hugh had fallen on the floor and was rocking and tumbling around the corridor as if he was on a whirligig.

"Your face!" he screamed, renewing his hysteria by the mere mention of it.

"What?" chuckled Lucy. Hugh gathered himself to speak.

"When you heard that noise . . . and thought there was some sort of monster in the room . . ." He fell backwards in a paroxysm of delight.

"Well?" said Lucy.

"It was the woman snoring!" he screamed again and, too exhausted to move or speak any further, he lay flat on his back and abandoned himself to his mirth.

Lucy's initial reaction was one of shock. To have reached such a pitch of excitement that she could mistake so ordinary a sound for something so fantastic! Secretly she had been rather proud of the way she had been coping. Now she could see what a tattered state her nerves were in.

She looked at Hugh – eyes closed, mouth like an underground tunnel, howling uncontrollably on the floor. A sentence, snatched from the past, flitted through her mind: "Honestly Lucy! Wolves in the cupboard! Sharks in the bath! You do let your imagination run riot!" She recalled the indulgent smile on her mother's face. With a great sense of release, Lucy felt the laughter rise within her and shoot into the air with the force of an uncorked bottle of champagne.

If those cries could have woken the woman from her slumbers, if she had had but the eyes to see, she might have discovered, in the corridor outside, two strange children rolling and roaring like lion cubs at play beneath the gloom.

Chapter Fourteen

As the last spasms of laughter died within them, Lucy and Hugh hauled themselves, exhausted but replenished, off the floor. Through the door they could see that the Dread Aunt was sitting, still slumped over the desk, her body moving perceptibly to the rhythm of her breathing which now sounded rather less sinister than Lucy had previously thought. Round her waist, attached to a belt, there hung a pouch about the size of a large wallet. As the Dread Aunt was leaning towards it, the pouch was dangling in mid-air. Lucy pointed it out to Hugh.

"I'm sure that was where she put the key to the cupboard," she whispered. "So maybe the brooch is in there as well." Hugh nodded in agreement.

"Come on then," he said, "what are we waiting for?" and together they crept softly into the room.

Having been accustomed for so many years to being as noisy or as quiet as befitted the occasion, it was difficult for Lucy and Hugh suddenly to get used to the fact that they couldn't be heard at all. They could have approached the woman with the clamour of a herd of elephants and it would have made no difference, except perhaps that Hugh might have enjoyed it a bit more. But it is hard to shake off the habits of a lifetime and right now tip-toeing seemed the most appropriate thing to do.

Evidently the Dread Aunt had been writing a letter. A pen was still balanced precariously between her fingers and at her side lay a piece of paper on which the words were inked in a cruelly elegant hand. It was addressed to Mr Brownlow Esquire, of Brownlow and Brownlow Solicitors. Lucy scoured it for any further information.

Dear Mr Brownlow,

Following the death of the owner of Morley Hall, I have decided to vacate the house and go abroad with my niece and nephew. The poor things are so pale and drawn and I am sure that they will benefit from the effects of a warmer climate. I regret therefore that I will no longer be requiring your services.

Yours sincerely
Alice Abbot

Lucy stared at the letter. Far from clarifying matters, it served only to puzzle her further. She had no doubt that the woman's expression of concern for the children was false. But if, as the letter suggested, the children's father had died, then where was their mother? And what was the real reason for the Dread Aunt taking them abroad? The only thing it did seem to explain was why the house was so bare. It must be on account of their moving out.

Lucy surveyed the Dread Aunt with revulsion. Even asleep, there was something about her presence which cast a shadow over Lucy's heart. She jumped back in alarm as the woman's eyes began to twitch and flicker nervously. But her breathing continued as monotonous and regular as before. Lucy shivered to think what dark thoughts were being dreamt inside that head.

"She's fast asleep!" whispered Lucy. Hugh looked at the pen and the paper beside the Dread Aunt's hand.

"Bit like me with my homework," he replied.

"I wonder what she was doing," continued Lucy. "Out in the garden so early . . ."

"Whatever it was, at least it's tired her out."

"Well we'd better move quickly, while she's still sleeping."

"Why?" responded Hugh rather cockily. "What can she do?"

"For a start," Lucy began. "If we do have to get the stuff off her while she's awake and moving around, then we'd be running the risk of a collision . . ." Lucy shuddered at the thought of her previous encounter and the memory of that searing heat. "And there's something else. Something I can't really explain. I mean, I know she can't see or hear us. But somehow, I still don't feel quite safe." Hugh looked immediately less self-assured.

"All right," he said, with sudden authority. "I'll do it."

He moved round the back of the woman to where the pouch hung poised like an apple about to be scrumped. His initial idea was to detach it completely from the belt. That way they could remove the things without the risk of waking the Dread Aunt. But on closer examination he discovered that the pouch was securely attached to a chain which in turn was looped around the belt. So the only way to separate the two was to undo the belt itself. Obviously that was impractical. The alternative was to take each thing, carefully and painstakingly, out of the pouch.

Hugh warmed to the challenge. This would be something glorious to recount to his friends at school! Such work required great skill and ingenuity – the kind of daring that was beyond belief – and nerves wrought only of the hardest iron or steel. He wiggled his fingers like a surgeon about to operate. Lucy raised her eyebrows like a person about to laugh.

"Careful!" she hissed, as her anxiety got the better of her mirth. Hugh winked at her nonchalantly and reached for the pouch. Pressing it open, he slipped his hand inside. His fingers closed over something hard and cold. It was the key. He removed it and handed it to Lucy. The Dread Aunt slept soundly on.

"Gently! Gently!" muttered Lucy under her breath. Hugh reached for the pouch once more.

"I can feel the brooch, but there's something in the way . . ." He took out a creased white envelope. "That's better!" He caught the brooch between the very tips of his fingers and tried to pull it out. But it was wedged right in the corner.

"It's stuck!" he cried.

"Come on!" urged Lucy.

Without pushing his hand right inside, Hugh was unable to get a firm grip. He started trying to work the brooch loose. It was the first time in his life he had regretted biting his fingernails. He forced his hand further inside the pouch, which tugged gently at the belt round the woman's waist. Suddenly her breathing altered its rhythm. The Dread Aunt was

71

stirring from her sleep.

Lucy watched in horror as Hugh, not daring to move, stood caught with his hand still inside the pouch. The woman shifted uneasily in her seat and lifted her head in a semi-conscious effort to rouse herself. Her breathing hissed snake-like through the air as she strayed halfway between a state of wakefulness and rest. She turned her face slowly towards Hugh. Lucy could just see the whites of her eyes, which gleamed bright and sightless beneath their heavy, fluttering lids. Then, like a bloodhound that has scented its prey, her body seemed suddenly to stiffen.

"Who's there?" she snarled, in a voice which commanded a reply. Lucy struggled with herself not to answer. Hugh opened his mouth to speak.

"It's – it's me. It's Hugh," he stuttered. The Dread Aunt cocked her head, as if straining for some sound beyond her normal hearing. Her eyes, no longer in danger of flickering open, were now shut tight with the effort of her concentration, which seemed to cast a deathly hush over the room. And all the while, Lucy could sense the dark brooding presence of the Dread Aunt's mind, which was seeking to discover their existence.

The silence was unbearable. Lucy held her breath, fighting to master the fear which was in danger of overwhelming her. She felt her mouth begin to open in the formation of a scream . . .

Then, as quickly as she had stiffened, the Dread Aunt unexpectedly relaxed. Lucy's scream turned swiftly to a sigh of relief. The woman's head nodded. The moment had passed. She yawned, hungry for sleep and spreading her arms across the desk she settled like a carrion bird back to its nest. Hugh drew his hand carefully out of the pouch and gave the brooch to Lucy.

"What did I tell you?" he said. "Nothing to it!" Lucy eyed him sceptically.

"Then why did you answer her? Why did you tell her you were there?" Hugh stared at his sister blankly.

"What are you talking about?" he said.

"The woman!" began Lucy. "When she woke up – she didn't need to see us, she could sense we were here!" She looked at her brother in amazement. "Don't you remember?"

Hugh grimaced for a moment, as if trying to catch the remnants of some fast forgotten dream. "Can't say I noticed," he answered. Then with a puzzled frown, he added: "I don't really remember much at all."

Lucy cast one final fearful glance over the hunched figure at the desk. She clasped the brooch tight inside her hand.

"Let's get out of here," she cried, grabbing Hugh by the arm. "I don't want to be around when she discovers those things are gone!"

And as the children crept like shadows towards the door, a fleeting image, as of two frightened thieves, stole in to disturb the woman's dream.

Chapter Fifteen

Despite her anxiety, Lucy felt a sudden lifting of her spirits as she passsed out of the room. Perhaps it was the mere removal from the Dread Aunt's presence, or simply the atmosphere which in the corridor outside now appeared somewhat less oppressive. She breathed deeply, in an effort to clear her head. But the air seemed only to half fill her lungs and again she got the horrible feeling that she was being slowly suffocated.

Lucy suddenly stopped as she felt something slip from her hand on to the floor. Looking down, she recognized the envelope that Hugh had handed her from the pouch. She had forgotten it even existed.

"Let me see that," said Hugh, bending down and snatching the envelope from under Lucy's nose. "This looks like the one she picked up from the desk – you know, when she walked right through you."

"Oh?" replied Lucy absently.

"Yes. Well you were too scared to notice, but she seemed very relieved to find it. It could be something important." Hugh sat down on the hall floor. Lucy stared at him in confusion.

"What are you doing?" she asked. Hugh had opened the envelope and was in the process of removing the contents from inside.

"Come on," said Lucy, shaking herself back to her senses. "We haven't got time." But Hugh had already unfolded several sheets of paper which he was studying with an unusual enthusiasm. His face flushed pink with excitement and he gestured triumphantly towards Lucy.

"Listen to this!" he cried. He began to read out loud.

"This is the last will and test-a-ment of David Adam Abbot! . . ." Hugh paused, his pride inflating like a balloon with the importance of his discovery. He waited for some acknowledgement from Lucy.

"Well go on!" she said, determined to inflate him no further. Hugh grinned idiotically and carried on reading.

"I here-by re-voke all form-er tes . . . test-a . . ."

"Let me see!" said Lucy, holding out her hand. Hugh snatched the paper away.

"No. I found it!" he declared, turning his back on his sister so she couldn't see. Lucy peered over his shoulder.

"It says 'testamentary'!" she announced. Hugh spun round and pushed her away.

"Get off!" he shouted. "Why do you always have to do everything?" He sat down facing Lucy and started to read the will quietly to himself, with the occasional loud exclamation of surprise calculated to annoy his sister. Lucy tried to pretend she wasn't interested, but in the end her curiosity got the better of her.

"All right," she sighed. "I'll listen while you read it out." Hugh smiled victoriously.

"No interruptions?"

"No interruptions!"

"Then I'll go on from where I left off," he said. Hugh began reading again. "I here-by re-voke all test-a-ment-ary dis-po . . . dis-po-si-tions made by me and de-clare this to be my last will. I app-oint my wife Margaret May Abbot to be the ex . . . ex-ec . . ." Hugh bit his lip in frustration. ". . . to be ex . . . ex-ecu . . . What's that?" he asked, pointing out the word to Lucy.

"Executor!" she replied.

"Oh! . . . What does it mean?"

"I think it means the person who carries out the instructions."

"Oh! . . . to be the executor of this my will. I give the whole of my estate both real and per-son-al to my said wife Margaret May Abbot with the ex . . . ex-cep . . . Why do they have to use so many words beginning with 'ex'?"

" 'Exceptions" said Lucy, cocking her head so she could see the paper.

". . . with the exception of the following . . ." Hugh paused. His whole face was furrowed with deep lines of concentration. He lifted up the paper to continue, then lowered it again. He had made his point. Now it was too much effort. He chucked the paper casually over to Lucy. "Here. You read it!" he said and leant forward on his elbows to listen.

Lucy smiled and, taking the will, she scanned it from top to bottom. The print was bold and clear and quite easy to read apart from the occasional word of which she could only guess the meaning. It was written in the dry formal style that adults seemed to reserve for matters they considered to be serious. To Lucy, it just sounded drab and rather dreary. The following page was largely concerned with specific items which were to be left to various individuals. There was nothing of real importance.

"I don't think this is going to tell us much," concluded Lucy, turning the page again. The list of items continued, after which there was a short clause in which it was stated that following the death of both parents the entire estate would be inherited by the children. From the little Lucy knew of such matters, there was nothing that seemed out of the ordinary.

She was just about to replace the will in its envelope when she noticed a passage at the bottom of the page which had been faintly underlined. She looked at it more closely.

"Hugh! Listen to this!" whispered Lucy excitedly. She began to read the passage out loud. "In the unlikely event of myself and my wife both dying while the children are still minors . . ."

"Miners!" said Hugh, screwing up his face. "I can't imagine their ever being miners!" Lucy stifled a giggle.

"Not miners as in people who work down mines!" she snorted. "Minors as in people who are under a certain age!" Hugh tried to pass it off as a joke.

"I knew that!" he answered, going rather red.

Lucy turned the page and continued. ". . . a trust will be set up for the benefit of the children. In this event I appoint my only sister Alice Eve Abbot . . ."

"That must be the Dread Aunt!" interjected Hugh.

". . . as the sole guardian and trustee. The children should have equal rights and if one child dies as a minor then the deceased child's share should pass to the surviving child. Should both children die as minors then the entire estate will be inherited by the guardian Alice Eve Abbot."

"I bet that's why she hates them!" cried Hugh. "Because they're stopping her from getting all the money."

"Probably," agreed Lucy. "Well let's hope they both live to be a hundred!"

"Is there anything else on the will?"

"Only some signatures. And a date I can't read. I think it's the same writing as on the back of the photograph." The memory of those faces seemed suddenly to fill them with an overwhelming sense of sadness.

"Do you think they're dead?" asked Hugh. "I mean Edward and Emily's parents?"

Lucy averted her eyes and gazed intently into space. The seconds seemed to swell to minutes.

"I suppose so," she answered finally. "Otherwise the Dread Aunt wouldn't have this will. And she certainly seems to be in charge of the children."

"They can't have known what she was like!" cried Hugh. "Or they never would have wanted her to look after them."

"Beware the smile of the crocodile," repeated Lucy to herself.

"What?" said Hugh.

"What was that rhyme? The one Mum used to tell us – about pretending to be something that you're not . . ." Lucy bowed her head, as if searching for something that was lost. Then, like a friend, it returned, and her brow cleared with the sudden recollection:

"Things are seldom what they seem
And skimmed milk masquerades as cream!"

Chapter Sixteen

Tucking the paper inside the envelope, Lucy scrambled to her feet.

"We're forgetting the children!" she cried in dismay. "All this time we've been sitting here talking, they've been locked up in that cold dark cupboard."

But Hugh wasn't listening. He stood motionless, staring distractedly up at the wall. Lucy tried to follow the direction of his gaze, but she could see nothing that might be attracting his attention.

"The picture . . ." murmured Hugh, without averting his eyes. Suddenly Lucy realized that he was staring at the blank spot on the wall where the picture used to hang. The one she had asked him about earlier.

"It was of the sea," he continued. "It was a picture of the sea in winter." Hugh turned away, a troubled sad expression on his face. Whatever emotion was tormenting him, he was struggling to find the words to express it.

"It'll always seem like winter in this place," he said.

An image of the picture flashed vividly through Lucy's mind. Once again she saw the waves, towering snow-capped mountains hurling the spray into a tumult as it hardened to crystals in the freezing air. She saw the steep slope of the shore, all frosted over, descending like an avalanche to the sea. And a single bird, buffeted high above the water by a cruel wind, searching for food amidst the frozen wastes. Lucy had always imagined she could hear its shrill, piercing cry.

The picture was so wild, so cold. It had always fascinated Lucy. She used to close her eyes and feel the force of the wind against her body and the taste of the salt upon her tongue. Strange that she should ever have forgotten it. And now that she remembered it again, it seemed to be calling to her of something else, something down in the hidden deeps of her memory, something she wanted to forget . . .

Disturbed and frightened, Lucy looked over to Hugh. He too was upset.

"What is it, Lucy? What is it that we don't understand?" Again Lucy felt the responsibility like a ton weight upon her shoulders. Straightening herself and forcing a smile on to her worried face, she said, "I don't know. It probably isn't important. I don't suppose we can expect to understand everything." Hugh looked a little comforted. It made Lucy feel stronger.

"We're forgetting the children again!" she said. "Come on," and she led the way across the hall and to the passageway beyond.

Outside the room, Lucy just caught the faint murmur of voices, which stopped when she opened the door. Somehow even the silence in the house was oppressive. Lucy thought wistfully of the calm, sweet quiet of the lake on a summer's day and the honeyed air which played about the banks. But here it was as if she was deep underground, in a cavern without ventilation, where the silence loomed heavy and ominous and waited patiently for something to happen.

"Do you think it'll help?" asked Hugh. "I mean, letting Edward and Emily out? It might just make the Dread Aunt worse."

"Perhaps," replied Lucy. "But we don't know how long she was planning on keeping them in there. We couldn't leave them locked up for days."

"It might frighten them," said Hugh. "To find the door open and no one there."

"Yes. But I bet it won't frighten them as much as being shut in that cupboard." Lucy paused. "All right?"

Hugh nodded as Lucy inserted the key and then twisted it in the lock. The door swung towards her with an eagerness which suggested it was glad to be open. There followed a short interlude in which nothing happened. Then there was a slight shuffling noise and first two hands, then a dark head, appeared timidly round the door. It was the boy. He turned back and called in a high quavering voice, "There's no one here. You can come out now."

Blinking and startled by the sudden light, the children emerged. They glanced nervously around, seeming to sense some trap. Their eyes swam large and dark with fear. Then, with one swift movement, they ran towards the door and vanished as suddenly as if they had never been there at all. Lucy stared after them.

"I wonder what they were doing the first time we saw them," she mused. "Wandering round the house as if they were in some sort of trance."

"Perhaps they were sleepwalking," suggested Hugh.

At that moment a thin screech rose as if from nowhere, clawing at the air like fingernails down a blackboard, then trailing off again into the silence. Lucy felt an icy shiver run down and freeze her spine. She didn't need to guess the cause of that frightful cry. She knew instinctively what it was. Hugh looked up at her, his brows knit with the anxiety of one who doesn't understand.

"It's the Dread Aunt," wailed Lucy. "She's discovered those things are gone!" She felt her brother stiffen at her side and the sharp jab of his knuckles as he clenched his fists. Outside, Lucy could hear the unmistakable sound of footsteps hurriedly crossing the hall.

"She's coming in here!" she yelled, her voice rising to a pitch of hysteria. And with all that was left of her reason, Lucy took the envelope containing the will and threw it on the floor.

The door burst open with the force of a hurricane and the Dread Aunt stood, even taller than Lucy remembered, her red hair dishevelled and blowing out behind as with the breath of some unearthly wind. Her whole frame seemed to glow as if lit by a flame within. She glared at the cupboard and the door, which gaped open, in an expression of dismay. She drew a sharp intake of breath as her mouth curled in undisguised astonishment.

"So! The little fledglings have flown their cosy nest!" Her voice sizzled and scalded the cold air. "But how?"

She twisted her head to inspect the room. Her glance fell immediately upon the envelope, which Lucy had discarded on the floor. Eagerly, she bent to pick it up. The static crackle of her skirt reminded Lucy of dead sticks upon a fire.

Suddenly with an almost imperceptible quiver, the woman stiffened and closed her eyes. Her arms were stretched in front of her, one hand still clutching the envelope, the other curled as if round some invisible object. Then slowly the fingers on her free hand straightened and, feeling their way through the air, worked gradually round the room until they stopped several metres in front of the spot where Lucy and Hugh were cowered against the wall. Trusting to some dark and deadly intuition, with her eyes still shut, the Dread Aunt started walking towards them.

"Who is it?" she crooned, in a soft milky voice. It had a strange hypnotic quality. "Who's there?"

Lucy started towards the door.

"Don't go!" said the woman. "I won't hurt you."

Lucy stopped reluctantly, as her limbs became unbearably heavy. Beside her, Hugh stood transfixed, his eyes glazed, his face a mask of blank submission. Again, Lucy felt the force of the Dread Aunt's will, like a great weight bearing down upon her, crushing the breath from her body and urging her to yield to some dark command. She struggled with herself not to give in. It was as if she was under water, fighting to get back to the surface, but sinking lower and lower as she gasped for air.

"Whoever you are . . . whatever you are . . .," cooed the Dread Aunt. Then, anticipating her conquest, she relaxed. "I'll teach you to meddle in matters that don't concern you!"

The abrupt change in her voice shocked Lucy back

into her senses. The Dread Aunt was almost upon them. Lucy nudged Hugh desperately hard in the ribs, but he remained unmoved. She pinched his leg, mercilessly increasing the pressure until, with a horrible yelp, he started up.

"What did you . . .?" he began, but a sharp jolt to his shoulder stopped him mid-flow. Just as the woman's hand smacked against the wall, in the exact spot where Hugh had been standing, Lucy pulled him out of the way.

Immediately the woman turned and began once more to move towards them, her speed growing with her agitation and the knowledge that she had let her advantage slip away. Lucy and Hugh edged frantically round the wall towards the door. As if guessing their intentions, the Dread Aunt cut a path direct across the room. With a surge of panic, Lucy realized she was going to block off their retreat.

"Now!" she cried and mere seconds before the woman reached the doorway, Lucy managed to push Hugh through. As she tried to follow, the Dread Aunt turned and with her arm made a wild lunging grab which caught Lucy on the shoulder. A searing pain burned its way like a fuse wire down her back and held her motionless for as long as the woman's hand was in contact with her body. But momentarily confused, sensing that something was happening but not quite sure what it was, the Dread Aunt withdrew her hand and so released Lucy from her hold. Lucy tumbled into the passageway, where Hugh pulled her hurriedly to her feet. Together, they raced towards the hall.

Unable to resist the urge, Lucy cast one final glance behind her. The Dread Aunt was standing out in the corridor, her figure made more ghastly by the surrounding gloom. Her eyes, which were now wide open, were staring at a point just above Lucy's head. At least she couldn't see them – not now, not yet.

Lucy turned away, not able to endure the sight for longer. But there was nothing she could do to stop the sound. The words which assailed her ears, she was powerless to resist.

"You might have escaped me this time," laughed the woman. "But you won't be so lucky the next!"

Chapter Seventeen

Down the corridor and across the hall, Lucy and Hugh bundled through the first door they came to. They found themselves back in what in their time they used to call the playroom. Now it was piled high with old dusty newspapers, parched yellow by age and by the sunlight which was shining over everything with a refreshing brilliance. Over in the far corner of the room were stacked a few ancient boxes and trunks that reared towards the ceiling like a rickety staircase.

Hugh sat down on the edge of a box and buried his face in his hands.

"Don't worry," said Lucy. "We'll make sure it doesn't happen again." Hugh tutted and shook his head.

"It isn't that," he said.

"Then what is it?" asked Lucy surprised. There was a pause as with an impatient gesture, Hugh rammed his foot against the box. His brow was furrowed with anxiety.

"The will!" he exclaimed at last. "Why did you chuck it on the floor?" Lucy hesitated, unsure of the cause of his consternation.

"Because I thought the Dread Aunt might be able to see it, as it doesn't belong to us. That would have been a dead giveaway – an envelope floating around in mid-air!" Hugh remained unconvinced.

"Well I think we should have kept it," he said.

"Why?" asked Lucy. Hugh clenched his fist and knocked it against his forehead in frustration.

"As evidence!" he cried. "Don't you see? When we get back to our own time, no one will believe us! They'll all think we've just made it up." Lucy stared at him incredulously. Trying to follow her brother's train of thought was like trying to follow an overgrown track, which wound and twisted and doublebacked and disappeared and sprung up somewhere else, but never led anywhere.

"Then don't tell them!" she replied. Hugh gawped at her. This time it was his turn to be amazed. What was the point, he asked himself, of doing heroic deeds if you couldn't tell anyone about them? He closed his eyes and tried to recapture the past vision of his glory. But now the ring of faces which encircled him were all sneering and twisted with scorn. And overshadowing everything were the greatly magnified heads of Beefy Keith and Spiky Isaacs, laughing and crying out in loud derisive voices: "Liar! Liar! Liar!" Hugh opened his eyes and to his relief, the vision disappeared.

However irrational she thought her brother to be, Lucy was still sorry to see him so upset. "We'll find something," she tried to console him. "I mean, as proof that we've been here." Hugh nodded and continued to stare despondently at the floor.

Shielding her eyes, Lucy moved over to the window. The sun, which had moved lazily on into the afternoon, now gazed directly down upon the back of the house. Far off on the horizon, Lucy thought she could detect a faint puff of smoke, trailing grey against the bleak winter sky. She wondered where it had come from. Time past or present? An old forgotten farmhouse? A factory from long ago? Or perhaps it was the spume of a jet plane. Or a whiff from the fire in Mrs Latter's kitchen – both cheering indications that their own world still existed. Lucy looked at the hedge which ran round the edge of the grounds and tried to envisage the barrier which closed them in. When, if ever, would they be released? Was there some plan, some task to be completed first? Where was the end to all this?

Turning away, she picked up one of the newspapers from the floor. Hugh was now gazing blankly at the wall.

"Hey! Bet this is old!" enthused Lucy, shaking the newspaper in an attempt to grab her brother's attention. To her surprise, Hugh jumped up with a start.

"Lucy!" he cried. She hadn't bargained on awakening such an interest.

"Look at this!"

Suddenly Lucy realized that it wasn't the newspaper that was exciting him at all. Dropping it on the floor, she crossed the room to where her brother was pointing towards a large chip in the skirting board.

"What do you think of that?" he exclaimed. Lucy didn't quite know what to say.

"Don't you recognize it?"

"No," she replied.

"It's the mark I made with my skateboard," said

Hugh. "Don't you remember? Mum was so angry she confiscated all my football magazines."

"But it can't be!" answered Lucy.

"It is. Look! It's in the shape of a sort of 'L'. I remember because I thought of blaming you. Saying you were trying to carve your name in it or something."

"Oh thanks!" said Lucy. "Anyway, it can't possibly be the same mark." Suddenly she laughed. "It must have been there already! Just think, Hugh – all those wasted football magazines for something you didn't even do!" Hugh scowled but before he could answer there came a loud crash from the hallway.

"What was that?" he hissed.

"Sounded like the front door," responded Lucy. They both hesitated, not wanting to act. At last it was Hugh who spoke.

"We'd better go and check," he said. Rather reluctantly, they sneaked across the room and peered round the doorway. The hall was empty. There was no one there.

"Do you think it was someone coming in or going out?" whispered Lucy.

"Going out, I hope," answered Hugh.

Crouching like soldiers under fire, they passed along the hallway to the window by the front door. Outside, they could see no sign of life or movement. And the snow, which once again was falling thick and silent, would have muffled any but the strongest sound.

It was then that Lucy noticed, some way over to her right, a streak of fiery colour standing out against the sky. Immediately it disappeared, then reappeared seconds later. As Lucy watched, the pattern was repeated over and over, flickering like a danger warning from afar.

The image worked in flashback through her mind. Suddenly it was as if she was back in her bedroom, looking out and seeing the Dread Aunt for the very first time. Except that now her vantage point was that much closer. And as the woman stood with her back towards them, as the spark of her hair seemed to come and go with the endless movement of her task, Lucy was actually able to see the mound of earth piled high amongst the bushes and the spade which she held in her hands.

A sense of dark foreboding began to overshadow Lucy. Tearing herself away from the window, she dodged round her brother and heaved the front door open. It creaked and groaned in protest.

"Wait here!" she cried. And before Hugh knew what was happening, the door had clicked softly shut. He watched anxiously through the window as Lucy swerved off to the left, then started to sweep round in a wide arc to a point which brought her level with the woman. Cautiously, she began to advance towards her, creeping, stealing, closer and closer. While the woman worked on and on, her camouflage spoilt only by her hair, which blazed and glimmered against the winter's fleece.

A helpless spectator, Hugh observed the scene, his hopes and his fears shifting with the frequency of his gaze, which turned from one distant figure to another. Any moment he expected to see the Dread Aunt stiffen, to cease her work, to show some indication that she had sensed his sister's approach. But as both figures gradually came within direct scope of his vision, Hugh was surprised to see, not the woman, but Lucy, stop and suddenly go rigid. They could only have been about ten metres apart – the Dread Aunt, toiling endlessly up and down and Lucy, frozen less, it seemed, by the temperature than by some unknown fear.

Hugh cried out, frightened lest his sister be discovered. And at the same moment, whether by coincidence or whether stirred by some distant perception of her brother's anguish, Lucy broke free of her frozen mould and started running back towards the house. From that distance, Hugh could only imagine the expression on her face. But the panic which drove her on was clear to see. While her arms thrashed as wildly as if she was drowning, while her head was tilted back and she strained for breath. Hugh wondered, with ever increasing alarm, from what horrible discovery she was fleeing.

He opened the door just as Lucy reached the porch. Her eyes, which were rolling partly with fear and partly with the exertion of her run, gave her ashen face a half-deranged appearance. She staggered into the hallway and leant back on the door with a force that slammed it shut. A rush of freezing air sliced like a razor through Hugh's frame.

Lucy slid, exhausted and wretched, to the floor. She sank her head on to her knees in an effort to regain both her breath and her composure. Her shoulders heaved and jerked in a feverish rhythm.

"What was she doing?" cried Hugh. But Lucy could not catch her breath enough to answer. Too desperate to care more for her distress, Hugh bent down and shook Lucy by the shoulders.

"Tell me!" he cried again. "Tell me what you saw!"

With her head still bowed, Lucy gathered herself to speak. The reply came as if from nowhere, like a disembodied curse.

"She was digging two graves," she said.

Chapter Eighteen

"But why should she want to kill us?" wailed Hugh.

The hall echoed to the thin tune of Lucy's wheezing as she struggled to regain her breath. She couldn't understand why it was taking so long. It was as if the air didn't want to fill her lungs.

"Not us!" she gasped and had to stop. She was inhaling so deeply that it was making her dizzy. She leaned further towards the floor and felt the rush of blood to her head. Finally, she began to recover. "Not us!" she repeated at last.

Lucy sat up and looked her brother full in the face. She was still pale, but there was nothing grey about her pallor now. And her voice was quiet and restrained, with only the faintest trace of a tremor to betray anything of her recent ordeal. "The graves are for Edward and Emily," she said.

Hugh stared at her, his expression changing as fast as his emotions. The fear which he had felt on his own behalf, now stirred to a mixture of horror and indignation on behalf of the twins.

"How do you know?" he asked. "Even if they are graves, how do you know that they're meant for Edward and Emily?"

"First, going by the size and shape of them, they couldn't be anything else," replied Lucy. "And second, it all makes sense. That letter . . ."

"What letter?" interrupted Hugh.

"There was a letter on the Dread Aunt's desk," Lucy explained. "I read it while she was asleep. She'd written to a solicitor to tell him that she was taking the children abroad . . ."

"So why should she be digging two graves?" asked Hugh.

"Because that letter was just a cover!" cried Lucy. "So as not to arouse anyone's suspicions. No one will miss the children if they think that they're abroad. And when the Dread Aunt returns, she can say that something awful happened and the children were killed while they were away. So no one will think of looking for them here!"

"Then all she has to do is collect the money!" added Hugh. He clicked his fingers with the sudden revelation. "So that's why there are no servants round the house! She couldn't risk anyone else finding out."

"Exactly!" Lucy replied. "And that's why she insisted that the children stay inside."

Lucy sat back and smiled quietly to herself. Now that the shock had subsided, she felt calmer than she had since the day began. It was the sudden comfort of knowing – after interminable hours of fearful speculation – the rush of relief which comes when a mystery is solved. Despite the seriousness of their predicament, at last she understood why they were there. It was like the lifting of a deep dense fog, although somehow, somewhere, Lucy had the vaguest sensation of a mist which enshrouded her still . . .

"We have to stop the Dread Aunt!" she declared. Hugh didn't respond. He was lost in thought. Looking at him, Lucy could see that he too was somehow more relaxed, composed. Up until then, it seemed they had been pouring their energies like water down a bottomless well. Now they had some basis, something concrete on which to act.

"We need to think about this carefully," Hugh began. Lucy glanced up in surprise. It was unusual for Hugh to think at all, let alone be careful about it.

"All right," she said. "Go on."

"Well," continued Hugh. "We know that the Dread Aunt is able to sense when we are there. And it would seem that the only way to stop her harming Edward and Emily is by harming her ourselves . . ."

"Unless we try and lock her up," suggested Lucy.

"But how? And for how long?" Lucy shrugged her shoulders. It was a relief, for once, not to have to do all the thinking. "No," said Hugh. "We need something a bit more permanent."

"All right," said Lucy. "What?"

"As I was going to say," Hugh went on. "Knowing the power she has, it would be useless trying to stop her from doing anything ourselves . . ." He paused, partly to gather his thoughts and partly for effect. "So I suggest we don't try to stop her at all!"

Lucy gaped at her brother in dismay. She might have known it was a mistake leaving all the brainwork to him. "So what *do* we do?" she cried.

Hugh smiled triumphantly. "We warn Edward and Emily instead!"

With a start, Lucy realized that her brother was

actually making sense. She signalled to him to continue.

"It'll be much easier for Edward and Emily to escape from the Dread Aunt than for us to try and stop her. Especially if the Dread Aunt doesn't even suspect what they're up to."

"Ah!" replied Lucy. "But what about the barrier round the house? How are they going to escape?" Hugh grinned confidently once more.

"You're forgetting one thing!" he said. "This is *their* time not *ours*. They shouldn't have any trouble getting out!"

For the sake of her brother's modesty, Lucy tried to conceal her admiration. She failed miserably. Hugh swaggered visibly as in her mind's eye Lucy watched his head swell to the size of a pumpkin.

"OK," she said eagerly. "How do we do it?"

"What?" muttered Hugh, still basking in the reflection of his glory.

"How do we warn Edward and Emily?" Lucy asked. Hugh blinked several times and looked suddenly less self-assured.

"Oh!" he said, his face reddening. "Oh that!" Lucy eyed him with impatience.

"Well?" she prompted. Hugh gestured defiantly.

"I can't be expected to think of everything!" he snapped. Lucy didn't know whether to laugh or cry.

"Hugh!" she wailed. "That's the main part of your plan!"

"Well, you think of something," he grumbled and removing the chewing gum from his pyjama pocket, he kicked it dejectedly across the floor.

Lucy sat back and tried to rack her brains for an idea. But nothing of significance occurred. She wondered whether she could have been mistaken, whether the reason for the Dread Aunt's digging was actually far less sinister than she had thought. But then she remembered all the other things: the will, the Dread Aunt's hatred of the children, the letter which lay unposted on her desk . . .

"I know," cried Lucy excitedly. "We'll send them a note! We can't speak to them. And they can't see us. But there's nothing to stop us writing . . ." and with that she jumped up and disappeared down the passageway in the direction of the dining room. She returned about a minute later, clutching a piece of paper and a pencil in her hand.

"Funny that we should have to borrow her stuff to do it," she mused.

Lucy settled back down on the floor and spread the paper flat. "What shall we write?" she asked. Ignoring, for once, the prickings of his jealousy, Hugh rallied to her support.

"Something that will frighten them enough to make them want to escape," he replied. "But not so much as to leave them helpless with fear!"

"OK," said Lucy. "Listen to this," and she started to scribble something down: "Edward and Emily! You don't know us but we are writing to you as friends. You are not safe in this house with your aunt. You must escape and find someone who can help you. Tell them everything that has happened. There is a spot in the garden, to the right of the house, where there is a small clump of the bushes. Take them there . . ."

Lucy looked over to her brother. He nodded his approval. Lucy folded the paper.

"Now we just have to find out where they are," she said.

"I think I heard them go upstairs. They might still

be there," suggested Hugh.

"All right," replied Lucy. "We've got to start somewhere," and she began clambering up the stairs to the corridor above. Outside the wind was rising once again. It whistled and howled round the house with a force that suggested it was trying to get in. Lucy huddled deep inside her dressing gown. It was cold enough inside as it was.

Reaching the top of the stairs, she looked along the corridor to where the dark edges and sombre colours of the portraits added their cheerless contribution to an already dismal scene. On the floor the two coffin-like chests stood as stark reminders of the graves outside. As Lucy paused, and waited for her brother to catch up, she heard, or imagined she heard, high above the wind, a distant cry, like a human lament. At first, she thought it might be the children weeping. But as she strained to catch a second instance of the sound, she discovered that it was voices singing – sad, childish voices, clear and pure, lifted in innocent refrain. And there was something familiar about the tune. With a surge of emotion, Lucy realized that it was a Christmas carol.

Beside her, Hugh stood alert and poised, his every nerve thrilling with the sensation of the song. "It's coming from up there!" he cried.

They moved further along the corridor, drawing ever nearer to the voices, which every now and then would falter and die to nothing on the air, only to start up again with a disturbing urgency. Over and over the tune was repeated, gaining in pace and in volume what it lost in the quality of its beauty.

Lucy stopped outside their bedroom. The carol, which had become a frenzied chant, was now barely recognizable and there was something nightmarish about its change. Lucy closed her eyes, imagining the frail faces of the singers and the suffering which lay behind their song. Bending down, she began to push the note under the doorway opposite. It met with a moment's resistance, then slipped easily through.

She knocked twice and stepped hurriedly back against the wall. Immediately the desperate chorus ceased. For a moment, Lucy expected it to be resumed. But it hung incomplete in the heavy silence which once more governed the house. Seconds, minutes ticked by in which nothing happened.

"They must have seen the note by now!" whispered Hugh. "They must have read it."

As if to confirm what he had said, the door of the room clicked softly open and the twins stood, china-white and trembling behind it. They looked, first to the left, then to the right. And then they fled, like two frightened urchins from the scene of a crime.

Chapter Nineteen

"We've done it!" shrieked Hugh. "They're free!"

"So long as they get past the Dread Aunt," added Lucy. Hugh clapped his hands in delight.

"They'll get past her!" he cried. "She's too busy digging the graves to notice that there'll be nobody to put in them!" and he laughed, almost maniacally. Lucy breathed deeply and waited for the same sudden jubilation to hit her as it had done Hugh. But all she felt was a dull, empty ache. She could hardly believe it was all over.

"So what shall we do now?" piped Hugh. He was hopping around the corridor like a demented giant flea.

"Everything should go back to normal – seeing that we've done what we came for. Wait till I tell everyone at school!" and he roared up and down the corridor as if he had just scored a goal.

Lucy stood with her back to the wall and stared blankly into the room from which the twins had recently emerged. The door had been left half open. Through it she could just see the ends of two wooden bedsteads and an old-fashioned washstand, which was pushed up in front of the window at the far end. As usual, the floor was bare apart from a worn rush mat by the doorway, presumably to stop the draughts. In the absence of any other carpets or rugs about the place, it particularly attracted Lucy's attention.

"Of course, I still haven't got any evidence," declared Hugh, with a momentary check to his exultation. "Still, I suppose I could always invent some!" and he brightened again immediately. Then, with a sudden shout of alarm, he added: "Lucy! We must get into the bedroom! If everything changes while we're still out here – we might never get back!"

But Lucy didn't answer. She was down on her hands and knees peering at the mat in the doorway opposite. Hugh pounced and grabbed her by the arm.

"Come on!" he screamed. Lucy tried to pull away, but Hugh had her locked in a vice-like grip.

"Hugh! Wait!" She lunged towards the floor and snatched a piece of paper from underneath the mat. She flicked it open in her hand. "Look! Look what it is!" she yelled.

But Hugh, consumed with panic, was deaf to her appeal. "Come on!" was all he could cry.

Mustering all her strength, Lucy stood up and, taking hold of her brother by both arms, she shook him until his teeth began to rattle.

"Hugh! Listen to me!" she screamed. Gradually he started to calm down. "Look!" said Lucy, holding up the paper in her hand. "It's the note. They didn't get it."

"W-what?" stammered Hugh.

"It was caught underneath the mat," she said.

Hugh stood, all his joy and all his desperation frozen in that single moment of discovery. Lucy hated herself. She stared at the note in her hand. Perhaps she should have ignored it – pretended it wasn't there. But then she thought of the twins . . .

"But . . . why did they run away?" faltered Hugh.

"I expect because we frightened them," answered Lucy. "First, letting them out of the cupboard. Then knocking on the door. They were bound to be scared when they found there was no one there!"

"Perhaps they hid the note there after they'd read it," suggested Hugh.

"Hugh!" said Lucy firmly. "They didn't get it." Hugh nodded dejectedly.

"Anyway," added Lucy, trying what little consolation there was left. "I'm not sure it would have worked even if they had got it. The Dread Aunt said she'd punish them if they went outside. And they're more afraid of her than of anything." Lucy felt her eyes drawn irresistibly towards the portrait further along the wall. Perhaps it was where she was standing, but there was no longer even the pretence of a smile about the Dread Aunt's parted lips. It seemed rather as if her teeth were bared, like an animal about to attack.

"So do you think the twins are still inside the house?" asked Hugh.

"Probably," Lucy replied. They looked at each other helplessly. What more could they do? Lucy slumped to the floor, the last spark of her energy burnt through. She felt the cold gnawing like a maggot at her insides. Next to her, Hugh stood propped against the wall, his head bowed, his arms hanging limply down. Lucy struggled momentarily. Her eyelids weighed heavy as iron and threatened to close. She yawned and felt a horrible creeping torpor setting in . . .

As if from the very bowels of the house, there came a low sonorous rumble. It built to a quick crescendo and burst forth into the air with the slow, sad clarity of a single chime. Again it came, and again and again, twelve times in all, rousing Lucy from her stupor and singing in its deep base voice of the hours which ticked endlessly by. Lucy rubbed her eyes and jumped up in surprise.

"It's the grandfather clock!" she cried. "It's started!" She was seized by a surge of panic, unsure how long she had lain inactive on the floor.

"Quick Hugh!" she yelled, poking her brother hard as she ran past. "We've got to do something before it's too late." Hugh sprang suddenly into action and followed his sister down the passageway. He felt her own sense of urgency begin to infect him like a fever.

"What? What can we do?" he shouted after her.

"I don't know," called Lucy in desperation. "Something! Anything!" She tried recklessly to form some plan of action. But all she could see was the impassive face of the grandfather clock and all she could hear, long after it had finished, was its **slow**, steady chime, rolling, booming, reminding Lucy that time was running out. She reached the hallway and stopped, paralysed by indecision.

"Perhaps we should look for the children again," suggested Hugh. "Find some other way of warning them." He started at the sound of his own voice. It was pinched and thin, as if the cold had somehow taken hold of it.

"No!" said Lucy, with sudden authority. "It would take too long. We have to face the Dread Aunt

. . . distract her attention . . . play for time . . ." The very mention of the word renewed her panic. With mounting trepidation, she thought of Edward and Emily and wondered whether it was already too late.

"Then what?" cried Hugh, realizing the shortcomings of her plan. But Lucy didn't reply. She simply opened the door and sped off in the direction of the graves which, with a quaking heart, she feared might no longer be empty.

Chapter Twenty

Heedless of the danger, Lucy ran frantically towards the spot from which, not long before, she had just as frantically departed. But it was only to discover that the Dread Aunt had already gone. Lucy cast one sickening glance over the graves, which opened like hungry jaws out of the ground. She heaved a sigh of relief. They were as starved and as bare as the rest of that desolate surround. Hugh came running up behind.

"The Dread Aunt's not here," breathed Lucy.

"Well it's easy enough to find her," he gasped. "Just follow those tracks." He pointed to where a trail of long, thin footprints swung off in the direction of the gate. Without a moment's hesitation, Lucy began to follow in the Dread Aunt's wake.

The afternoon was drawing steadily to a close and in the deepening light the landscape lost something of its sparkle and took on a dull off-whitish hue. But Lucy, who had long become immune to the winter's charms, was only thankful that, as she studied the tracks, the snow had ceased to dazzle her with its glare. She barely noticed the waning sun as it streaked and coloured the sky, or as it settled here and there about a tree or ragged bush with a ghostly incandescence. And even had she noticed, so fixed was her purpose that she hardly would have faltered in her stride. Behind her, Hugh was having difficulty keeping up.

The tracks led her directly to the gate, where they veered off at a right angle along the line of the hedge towards the lake. Several paces further on they stopped, and although the reason for this was unclear, the snow was so trampled underfoot that it was obvious the Dread Aunt had not merely hesitated, but had lingered for some time.

As Lucy picked up the trail again, the pattern was repeated. For several metres the footprints would continue straight along the line of the hedge, then they would stop. Apart from that there was no real regularity to the movement. As far as Lucy could see, the stopping places were random and the distances between inconsistent.

Lucy wondered whether Hugh had been wrong, whether the Dread Aunt had been trying to get out and, like themselves, had failed. Tentatively, she stretched out her hand to the furthest side of the hedge. But when it got halfway, she found she could push it no further. It was the oddest sensation, odder still because Lucy couldn't actually feel anything. Whatever was stopping her, it had no temperature, no texture. It was merely a resistance, which paralysed any attempt at forward movement, while to move backwards was like a release. Lucy withdrew her hand. It was as she had suspected. The barrier still existed.

As she turned away, something deep and glistening at the side of the tracks caught Lucy's eye. In the gathering dusk it seemed to shine out at her with the rich resplendence of a tiny ruby. She bent down eagerly to pick it up and recoiled in horror as, on closer examination, she discovered not as she had expected, some small bright trinket, but a wine-dark stain whose only substance was in the manner of its clotting. Lucy looked round in alarm. The stains were everywhere, spattered across the snow like red ink from a fountain pen. Something seemed to twist and buckle inside her.

"No!" she screamed, in an agony of despair. Immediately, Hugh was by her side.

"What is it?" he gasped. "What's wrong?" Lucy pointed to the sinister drops on the ground.

"I think we're too late," she said. Hugh maintained his composure.

"No" he replied. "You could be wrong. It might not be what it seems." He searched around for the tracks. They had turned away from the hedge and were leading back towards the house.

"Look!" he cried, screening his eyes against the glow of the setting sun. "There she is! Over there!" Lucy followed the direction of his gaze to where the distant figure of the Dread Aunt cut a ghastly outline against the evening sky. Her bearing, usually so erect, was now somewhat stooped, giving Lucy the impression that she was carrying something. Beyond that, it was impossible to tell.

The sight of her roused Lucy's spirits. "Let's go!" she yelled. And this time Hugh was determined not to be left behind.

Lucy ran with her head bowed and her shoulders set against the freezing wind which bit into her

106

clothing and raged about her body with the fury of a wild beast unleashed. The light made it difficult to judge whether or not they were gaining any ground. Ahead of Lucy, everything was cast in shadow and the Dread Aunt appeared as a dark and deadly phantom, enticing, but for ever out of reach. Lucy lowered her head once more and, gritting her teeth, pressed on.

As they neared the house the sun sank gradually behind the roof and disappeared completely from their view. Immediately, Lucy felt the pressure on her eyes relax. She blinked several times before looking up. Now that she was in the shade, everything resumed its normal colour and perspective. She saw with a start that they had actually gained considerably on the Dread Aunt, who was now approaching the porch barely thirty metres ahead of them. As Lucy watched, the woman turned and with a murderous smile glanced back towards the bushes and the graves.

Lucy opened her mouth and waited for the scream which never came. For her terror had frozen her voice and the sound trailed as vapour from her lips, dispersing to nothing on the raw blue air. While the Dread Aunt turned her gaze from the graves to stare in horrible fascination at her outstretched hands. For whatever evil thing she had concealed, it now coursed from her palms into a thick red artery across the snow, and the white fur coat, no longer a camouflage, was smeared with its gory stains.

Chapter Twenty-One

As Lucy stared, transfixed with horror, the Dread Aunt disappeared inside the house. Hugh, who had been concentrating purely on keeping up, was totally unaware of what had happened. So he was suddenly surprised to discover that he had left his sister several metres behind. He started to run back to where she was standing, shouting at her to keep up. Somewhat stunned, Lucy followed her brother across the last lap leading to the porch.

The front door had been left half open. Inside, Lucy could just hear the soft timbre of childish voices.

"B-but we're not h-hungry, Aunt," they stammered, in trembling unison. Lucy swayed and clutched the pillar for support. It was more than she had dared to hope.

"They're still alive!" she breathed.

Meanwhile, Hugh stood on the threshold, straining for further snatches of the conversation.

"I gathered them especially," crooned the Dread Aunt, "to show you how much I care." Hugh frowned and signalled to his sister to come closer.

"C-couldn't we have them later?" pleaded the girl. There was a pause and the sound of a shoe, tapping impatiently against the floor.

"But you see, my dears," continued the Dread Aunt. "I went to so much trouble to collect them. And they won't last very long. So you should have them now – while they're still sweet and juicy." Again there followed a silence. Then the shrill falsetto voice of the boy: "But Mother told us we were never to eat such things!"

Lucy and Hugh looked at each other in confusion. Inside, a harsh rasping chuckle grazed the air.

"Well, Mother isn't here any more," hissed the woman. "So now you have to do what I say!"

That was enough for Lucy. She burst through the door just in time to see the Dread Aunt advancing upon the children. She started back in horror, perceiving the trick her imagination had played her yet again. The strange tracks along the hedge . . . the ominous red stains in the snow . . . all were explained by the cluster of berries which the Dread Aunt had clasped so tightly that the juice ran like blood from her hands.

"Hugh!" screamed Lucy. "She's trying to poison them!"

On the opposite side of the hall, Edward and Emily made a final desperate sprint towards the door. But the Dread Aunt whirled, and, swooping upon them with the full force of her fury, seemed to gain in her own stature what the cowering children lost in theirs, until she towered, huge and awesome, her arms outstretched, her hands dripping as if with the portent of their doom. As far as they could go, the twins backed off along the wall. Then huddling tight, they sank down in a corner, closed their eyes, and awaited their fate. With a flush of grim triumph on her face, the Dread Aunt closed upon them.

"Do something! Anything!" yelled Lucy. She frantically surveyed the hall. Over to her right, the grandfather clock looked placidly on, appearing to mock Lucy with its indifference. She rushed over and, taking hold of the panel at the back, tried to pull it forward from behind. But it was heavy and set so close to the wall that there was very little room for manoeuvre.

"Hugh!" she screamed. "Help me!" Grateful of the opportunity for action, Hugh half ran, half stumbled, across the hall.

"The other side!" cried Lucy. "Get hold of the back . . . now PULL!" But even with Hugh's help, the task proved no easier to accomplish. If Lucy hadn't been so near to hysteria, she would have sworn that the clock was deliberately resisting them. It stuck as fast as if it was rooted to the floor.

"Again!" shrieked Lucy. But still it stood, as firm and resolute as a sentry, and refused to move.

Lucy cast one final glance towards the children. Their tiny faces were shining ever whiter with their fear. But their hands, which held the berries high in an attitude of supplication, were already stained as if with the Dread Aunt's guilt.

"One last time!" breathed Lucy. And now as they pushed, as they strained every nerve and every muscle, as their whole frames shook with the exertion and the sweat shone like diamonds on their brows, the grandfather clock creaked and groaned and, with a sudden lurch forward, smashed into a thousand

110

tiny pieces at the Dread Aunt's feet.

The clock let out a final discordant twang, as if bemoaning its departure to the world. And in that moment it seemed to Lucy that time had indeed come to a standstill. For immediately the Dread Aunt turned and with a ghoulish smile looked across the generations which should for ever have divided them and saw Lucy and Hugh for the very first time.

Momentarily distracted from her hideous task, the woman advanced towards them.

"At last!" she seethed, and behind the malice there was an undisguised element of surprise. "And where have you come from . . . my dears?" The glass-blue eyes pierced Lucy like a blade of ice. Inwardly she shrank before their deadly glare, which outwardly rendered her powerless to move. Beside her, Hugh stared blankly ahead. He wore the glazed expression of one who has already submitted to the control of a stronger will.

For Lucy too the battle was almost over. The heat rose like smoke to cloud her thoughts and choke her resolution, which smouldered and died on the freezing air. Again she was aware of some clash in her sensations, some momentary conflict, as of two elements locked in a perpetual struggle. But as the Dread Aunt drew closer, the feeling of coldness passed and only the heat remained, growing for ever stronger, parching the inside of Lucy's mouth and setting her lungs on fire. The woman reached out, as her clothes spat and crackled like kindling and her flaming hair semed to ignite about her ghastly lurid face. And as she touched each child upon the shoulder, and this time maintained her hold, they became as two human infernos, raging with the heat of her fury and burning with the dark passion of her heart.

A fleeting image, of two children in terror-crazed flight, passed and blurred to nothing before Lucy's eyes. And then she began to sink down, down, further than it had ever seemed possible to go, into the murky unfathomable depths . . .

The last thing she remembered was the sound of rushing water overhead.

Chapter Twenty-Two

It was only seconds later when Lucy came to. She found herself huddled on the floor of the hall. Everything was still and somehow indistinct. Lucy felt numb and empty, as if all her emotions had been ripped out from inside. She couldn't remember what had happened. She even wondered if she might be dead.

"W-what shall we do now?" muttered Hugh, half in a daze. He was lying on his back staring distractedly at the ceiling. Lucy rubbed her eyes and attempted to sit up. But even that little movement made her feel sick. She was strangely hot and cold, as if she was running a fever. She dropped back on the floor and tried to concentrate. Despite her exhaustion, she again got the impression of something weighing heavy on her mind and on her body, rousing her and urging her into action. But what? What was it telling her to do?

On the other side of the hall a handful of berries

were crushed and scattered about the floor. While next to Lucy lay the sprawling remains of a grandfather clock which had fallen, like a soldier, face down in the mud. She felt the prick of broken glass beneath her hand and with a curious detachment studied the bright drop of blood upon her finger. It was as red and as round as the berries which littered the ground.

Lucy jumped up, forgetting her sickness in the fervour of her recollection. Of course! The Dread Aunt! Edward! Emily! The last thing she remembered seeing was Edward and Emily trying to escape. Lucy could only presume that the Dread Aunt had decided to forfeit herself and Hugh in order to chase the twins. Otherwise she very much doubted whether either of them would still be there.

Lucy ran to the front door and looked expectantly out towards the gate. There was nothing to be seen. She scanned the snow around and beyond the porch. And there they were, two sets of tracks, so tiny that they could have been mistaken for animals', with the occasional larger and deeper imprint, which ran over and threatened to obliterate them. As Lucy had expected, they headed off in the direction of the gate. But then, as if frightened, they swerved abruptly over to the left.

Lucy stared at the tracks and the point at which they deviated with an ever increasing alarm. And now she recognized that beyond her natural concern for the children's safety, there was an extra dimension to her fear. Suddenly it was as if all those events which Lucy had dismissed as unimportant, now crowded back to torment her: the dripping tap, the forgotten picture, the sense of sinking and of suffocation, the feeling that there still was something missing, something she didn't yet quite understand. And last of all she recalled her sudden and inexplicable aversion to the lake. The truth rocked Lucy with the cumulative force of an explosion. They were all warnings, all ghastly premonitions – of somebody drowning, of somebody's death!

Reluctantly, Lucy raised her head. At first, she hoped they might be her imaginings – the projections of her own worst fears. But as the figures moved on, and refused to fade, Lucy was forced to accept that they were real. Meanwhile, Hugh had recovered sufficiently to join her at the door.

"What's happening? Where are they?" he asked. Barely able to speak, Lucy tried to point the figures out. But her hand quivered like a leaf in the wind and, with a start, she noticed that the blood was still trickling from her finger. She dropped her arm hurriedly to her side and swallowed hard.

"They're heading towards the lake," she said. Hugh stiffened for an instant, as something deep within him also stirred. But impatiently, he pushed it to one side.

"We can still catch them!" he cried and he bounded out into the snow. Overhead, the sky was dappled red, providing a dramatic backdrop to the climax of the day. As Lucy ran, a sudden flash of light drew her attention towards the distant figures. They were skirting a difficult and dangerous path around the water's edge. Although it was impossible to gauge their speed, it was clear that however much of a lead Edward and Emily had started out with, the Dread Aunt was steadily gaining.

Lucy ran on, her breath rattling louder with each step. She stopped several paces from the edge of the lake and looked desperately across to the figures on the opposite bank. Their circuitous route had allowed Lucy and Hugh to gain some considerable ground, but although Edward and Emily seemed much less remote, there was no way of actually reaching them. And the Dread Aunt was closing on them all the time.

"We'll have to go across the lake!" cried Hugh, advancing nearer to the edge.

But Lucy rounded on him and with a strength which she had never before possessed, she hurled Hugh to the ground.

"No!" she screamed. Hugh gasped in horror as his sister stood, her eyes white and dilated in her livid face, her whole frame shaking as with some supernatural force.

A scream coming from the other side of the lake suddenly claimed his attention. He glanced across to where the Dread Aunt, now only a few steps behind the children, lunged wildly towards them. A sudden spark seemed to fire and die in her hand. At the same moment the children stumbled and, clutching each other in the blindness of their panic, slipped out on to the ice. On the verge of the lake, the Dread Aunt paused and with a ghastly flourish, held up her arm to the dying sun. There was a blinding flash, which streaked like lightning from her hand.

"She's got a knife!" shrieked Hugh. He glanced up from where he lay in the snow.

"It's too thin . . . ." Lucy muttered, over and over. "It's too thin . . ." Hugh stared at her, confounded.

"W-what?" he stuttered. Lucy turned slowly towards him.

"The ice . . .," she said. "It won't hold. It's too thin."

Hugh opened his mouth to contradict her. How

could she know that? How could she tell? But a voice from deep within him cried out and stopped the words. And suddenly Hugh knew that she was right.

Chapter Twenty-Three

Lucy and Hugh watched with grim anticipation as the children scrambled and skidded across the ice.

"Come back!" called the woman, her left hand hidden behind her. "I wasn't going to hurt you." But the sound of her voice only renewed their torment and Edward and Emily clasped each other tightly and struggled further towards the middle of the lake. While all round the wind began to quicken and something hard and smooth brushed against Lucy's cheek.

Tentatively, the Dread Aunt placed one foot over the bank to test her weight. Beneath her the surface felt comfortingly solid. She stepped down and stood uncertainly near the edge. But still the ice held firm and betrayed no signs or sounds of weakness. Gaining confidence, she took first one step, then another, towards the terror-stricken children. Then, with a thin smile, she strode purposefully across the lake to meet them.

The blade gleamed cold and blue in the Dread Aunt's hand, while her hair twisted and spiralled in the rising wind and licked about her head like tongues of fire. As Lucy shrank before the awesome sight, she again became aware of something touching her face, but now it seemed to tap and prod with the insistence of a long thin finger. Hardly daring to avert her eyes, she raised her hand to brush the thing away and cried out in pain as a sudden gust lashed it against her cheek. She reached up and caught hold of the trailing branch of a willow tree.

Immediately, there was a horrible groaning sound, as of something giving way under pressure, and Lucy looked back just in time to see Edward and Emily stumble and fall once more on to the ice. Already it was covered in a thin film of water, which was seeping through a gap in front of the children, making the surface even more treacherous underfoot. As they rose, then fell, there was another low moan, followed by a sharp bone-like crack, and more water began to spurt up behind.

Instantly the Dread Aunt stopped and with a laugh which seemed to lacerate the air, threw the knife high into the air, where it spun and sparkled like a catherine wheel. Then as it fell and hissed across the ice, she cautiously retraced her steps back towards the edge.

Lucy placed one foot against the trunk of the willow tree and began to climb. Overhead she could see that one of the boughs was broken and hung, like a half-severed limb, low over the surface of the lake. Its furthest branches nearly reached the spot where the twins crouched, shivering and wretched, in a pool of rising water.

"Hugh!" she yelled. "If this falls, get ready to

119

pull it to the edge."

Supporting herself on the branch above, Lucy began to kick at the broken bough. The main part of it had already torn away and the rest started to give slowly beneath the extra pressure. Out on the lake the ice continued to crack, threatening at any moment to give way. Lucy hauled herself up and jumped down with the full force of her weight. The bough splintered and crashed like a dismembered arm through the ice below. For a moment, Lucy was dangerously close to following it, as she dangled precariously in mid-air. But, swinging her legs around the trunk, she managed to clamber down.

Hugh leaned out and pulled the bough through the freezing water to the bank. The noise of its fall had attracted the twins' attention and they noticed, for the first time, the branches which trailed tantalizingly close to where they were stranded. The little girl stretched her hand uncertainly towards them and quickly withdrew it as the movement threw her temporarily off balance. She screamed and, clutching her brother by the waist, slid further beneath the surface of the ice. The sound of the Dread Aunt's laughter floated mockingly across the lake.

"Again!" breathed Lucy, her hands clasped in imitation of a prayer. "Please! Please! Try again!" As if in answer, the boy reached out his hand to the long, trailing fingers of the willow tree. Further and further, closer and closer, until he brushed the very tips of the branches but was unable to get a grip. Then as the ice beneath him rocked and finally gave way, he made a last desperate lunge and caught hold of the end of the furthest branch, while the girl still clung tightly around his waist. The bough lurched forward from the bank and Hugh grabbed it just in time to stop it moving out from the edge.

All around the children the ice had begun to break. Lucy and Hugh held fast to the bough which, now half afloat, rolled and pitched under the extra weight and threatened to offload the twins into the water, or worse, submerge them beneath the ice. But they clung as tightly to the tree as they did to each other and together they inched their way towards the edge.

From across the lake there came a piercing screech, like the shrill cry of a vulture. Lucy looked up to where the Dread Aunt stood several metres from the furthest bank. Even from that distance Lucy could detect the glitter of her eyes, which directed their malevolent gaze upon the escaping children. With a gesture of furious defiance, the woman turned completely round and took one step towards them. But her anger had conquered her caution, and as she placed her foot too firmly and too hurriedly on the ice, it twisted and slipped beneath her. There was a familiar crack, which accompanied the sound of her fall.

Lucy watched in horrible fascination as the woman struggled to get up. All around her the water was rising with an alarming speed. She clawed wildly at the ice, slashing it with her fingernails to maintain some sort of hold. But she succeeded only in scoring the surface.

Suddenly Lucy felt the pressure on the bough relax. She turned anxiously back to see Edward and Emily clinging mute and motionless, as if paralysed by the Dread Aunt's fall. Beside her, Hugh also had his gaze intently fixed upon the woman. United by their fear, and by a destiny which was somehow intertwined, all four children watched as the Dread Aunt struggled and thrashed and tried to outwit with her own foul nature the treachery of the ice. And as her role was so unexpectedly reversed, as she became no longer the attacker, but now the victim, the children wondered at the curious mixture of horror and relief in their hearts.

For a few seconds more the Dread Aunt floundered, hopelessly near to the edge. For a moment, it seemed that she might win, as she dragged herself for the last time to her feet and prepared to spring towards the bank. But with a sickening crash the ice all round her split asunder. The woman twisted herself to confront the children. Her entire frame was ravaged with a hideous rage, as she opened her mouth and with a scream that seemed to mutilate her face, declared some parting vengeance on the world. Then she threw up her arms in a gesture of ultimate challenge and vanished beneath the surface of the ice. The last thing Lucy saw was her hair – long, bright tentacles streaming out across the lake. Then that too disappeared, and descended like a monster, to the deep.

Far off on the horizon, the sky blazed an angry red. And with a dying spark which seemed to set the lake on fire, the sun bid farewell to the winter's day and sank behind the cover of the marsh.

Chapter Twenty-Four

Edward and Emily hauled themselves from the freezing water and on to the bank of the lake. Frightened and bedraggled, they gazed at the spot where the Dread Aunt had vanished, half expecting her suddenly to reappear. Their faces clouded with a dark uncertainty. They could hardly believe it was over.

It seemed a long time that they stood, staring silently out across the lake. Until finally, as if satisfied, they turned and without a word, started to run in the direction of the gate. They had gone only a few paces when, for no apparent reason, the little girl stopped and looked abruptly back, while the boy moved swiftly on. It was the first time Lucy had seen them act independently of each other. For a moment, she felt a vague warmth in the air as, with a puzzled frown, the little girl's eyes came to rest upon her own. But already her brother was upon her, tugging in gentle confusion at his sister's sleeve. She blinked and with a faint smile, turned her sweet face for ever from Lucy's view. Then together once more, the twins clasped each other's hands and hurried away.

Lucy and Hugh looked quietly on as the tiny creatures flitted across the snow and to the marsh beyond, then seemed to vanish like sprites into the air. For a few seconds more they lingered in silent reflection. They knew so little of those children, or the world in which they lived. And yet somehow, somewhere, Lucy felt there was a part of her which would always belong to them. Perhaps it was their struggle, their mutual fear, their common instinct for survival which forged some eternal bond. Whatever it was that the four children shared, Lucy sensed that at their parting something of herself left also and went to live for ever within the spirit of another time.

"Come on," she said at last. "We'd better get back inside the house." They walked quickly round the edge of the lake until they reached the end. So far they had followed in the twins' footsteps, but where they veered off in the direction of the gate, Lucy and Hugh turned and headed back towards the house. Their paths were different now.

The door was wide open, giving Lucy the strangest impression that it was actually inviting them inside. Despite the cold and the twilight gloom, the house seemed somehow less dismal, the air less heavy. But apart from that, everything remained the same. Exhausted, Lucy and Hugh clambered up the stairs and along the corridor to the bedroom. It was a relief to discover that, despite everything that had happened, at least nothing there had changed. It was all comfortingly familiar: the clock, the teddy bear, the bookshelf on which were stacked a few battered books and some chocolates, which Lucy had reserved partly for her own consumption and partly for bribing Hugh. Reaching up, she removed them from the shelf and offered Hugh the box. He shook his head.

"Not hungry," he replied. Lucy stared at him in surprise.

"Go on," she said. Hugh shrugged and, taking a chocolate, placed it indifferently in his mouth, whereupon he grimaced and spat it out across the floor.

"Ugh! Blimey, Lucy!" he cried, screwing up his nose in disgust. "How long have you had those?"

"Only about a week," she answered in some confusion.

"Yeah! And the rest!" he muttered crossly. He kicked the chocolate against the wall.

"Goal!" he murmured and flopped back on the bed.

Lucy smiled and, taking the clock from her desk, brushed off a surprisingly heavy layer of dust. She looked upon its face as she would upon a friend's. It was odd that it should suddenly have stopped, after so many years of never having stopped at all. She wound it up and listened as it whirred reluctantly into action. Its tick was slow and lazy, almost as if it couldn't be bothered to keep time. But at least it was actually working.

"What shall we do now?" asked Hugh, rapping his knuckles impatiently against the wall.

"Wait, I suppose," sighed Lucy. "What else?" She flung herself face upwards on her bed and thought longingly of her mother. It could only be a matter of time before they were reunited.

Seconds, minutes, hours seemed to pass as the children lay, confined to their room, and waited for the world to change around them. Every now and then, one of them would creep over to the door and peep out into the passageway. But always the same sombre portraits lined the walls and the wooden chests stood large and solid on the floor and appeared to taunt them with a horrible veneer of permanency.

"How much longer?" cried Hugh, slamming the door in vexation.

"Not long," said Lucy hopefully. "Not long."

She looked out to where the moon was rising ever higher in the sky, like a monarch laying claim to her dominion. As darkness loomed, it seemed to bring with it some change in the air, diffusing the bitter night chill with a warmth that was almost stifling. Again Lucy had the impression that she was somehow being suffocated. But now it was impossible to tell whether some haunting memory of the Dread Aunt's death or merely the weather was making it difficult to breathe. She walked over to the window and flung it open. But the atmosphere outside was equally oppressive.

Suddenly, through the darkness, Lucy saw a light shine out on the marsh. She narrowed her eyes in an effort to discern what it was. It gleamed with the steady orange glow of a torch and cut a welcome hole in the cover of the night. As Lucy watched, it seemed to come nearer to the house.

"Hugh!" she screamed. "Come here!"

The light was fast approaching the gate and Lucy could dimly see two shadows, one much larger and taller than the other, which seemed to skulk behind its glare. For one sickening moment, she thought the nightmare had started over – that these were just two more grim spectres come to haunt them from the past. But as she caught the faint murmur of voices deep in conversation, she realized, with a start, that there was something familiar about the sound.

Lucy peered intently through the darkness. The largest figure was evidently a man and, as far as she could tell, he was wearing some kind of uniform. Apart from that, there was nothing of particular interest. It was the other, smaller, figure which so attracted Lucy's attention. It was more hunched than she remembered, and under the torchlight the hair seemed to have lost all its remaining colour. But the walk! And the voice! And the features which, though indistinct, still blended in blurred resemblance! Lucy gasped in sudden recognition.

"Hugh!" she shrieked. "It's Mrs Latter!"

Chapter Twenty-Five

Had anybody tried to describe to Lucy the effect that her neighbour would one day produce, she would hardly have believed them. Never had a form seemed so lovely to her, never a face more dear! For now, at last, after a day which had spanned a lifetime, Lucy saw embodied in that slight and elderly frame a return, not only to her own world, but to the person who, above all others, she loved and cherished most. She closed her eyes and in her mind her mother reached out towards her.

Lucy leaned through the window and cupped her hands round her mouth.

"Mrs Latter!" she yelled. "It's me! Lucy! I'm over here!" To her surprise, the figure moved heedlessly on.

"Here! Over here!" she called again. But still Mrs Latter did not respond. She just strode purposefully off in the direction of the lake. Lucy turned to her brother, her brow drawn tight in confusion.

"Why can't she hear me, Hugh?" she asked. Outside the wind howled loud and the moon disappeared behind the gathering cloud, plunging the room even deeper into darkness.

"Something's happening!" Lucy cried out. "I can feel it in the air." Far off a noise, like the distant boom of a cannon, rumbled and shuddered across the marsh.

"It's a storm!" shouted Hugh, looking out upon the starless sky. "There's a storm brewing overhead!" As the thunder rolled ever nearer, Lucy clapped her hands to her ears.

"What's the matter?" shrieked Hugh, his voice high with excitement. "Don't you see? Mrs Latter ... the weather ... everything's changing! Going back to how it was before!"

But Lucy didn't respond. With her hands still covering her ears and her eyes shut tight in concentration, she tried to block out the sound of the storm. It wasn't that she was frightened. It was just that there was something else, something urging her to listen, something more that she wanted to hear ...

Suddenly it was as if she was outside, caught in the midst of the storm, while the wind buffeted and tossed her in its powerful arms and roared and raged inside her head. Listen to me! Listen to me! it seemed to cry. But still Lucy struggled to shut it out. Until at last a faint murmur broke like a burst of sunshine from deep within the tempest's heart. And as it rose and died and rose again, it seemed to ride the storm as a bird rides the wind, singing of the peace to follow after. Stronger and stronger, clearer and clearer, grew the sound, while all around the turmoil started to subside. Until finally, only the voice remained, warm and mellow in the aftermath of the storm.

"Lucy! Hugh!" it called.

Lucy choked back a sob. Was this the cruellest trick of her imagination? Or had Hugh heard it too? In search of an answer, she looked across to where her brother stood, his eyes awash with unshed tears. And as the voice called once again, lingering like a melody on the air, for the first time that day Hugh wept – and abandoned himself to the tide of emotion which he was no longer ashamed to show.

For one moment more, Lucy paused and drank the sound like nectar from the night. A surge of pure elation swept over and engulfed her, as she sprang up and headed towards the door.

"D-downstairs," she stuttered. "In the hall." Together they flew along the corridor, oblivious to the portraits which still hung like a silent chorus on the walls. All around them the darkness was lifting and the air, no longer stifling, was now refreshing in its warmth. And all the while the voice rang out, as clear as a bell on a bright blue morning, whose peals are the peals of laughter.

The children halted momentarily at the top of the stairs. And as they looked down upon the figure in the hall, it was as if all the chill and bitter memories of the winter's day began to melt in the heat of the sun. For with her hair gilded in the blazing light and her face flushed as with a summer's radiance, their mother surpassed even their fondest memories and stood, like a vision, before them.

As Lucy raced down the stairs to the hall, she could have sworn that her feet didn't even touch the ground. At last she was there! It was sweeter than her sweetest dream, more perfect than her wildest imaginings. All the years, all the responsibilities which had accumulated in a single day, now vanished beneath the soothing warmth of her mother's embrace. And Lucy was a child once more.

The muffled sound of Hugh's sobbing was all that broke the silence. Then that too died away. Together they stood, mother and children, clasping each other in blissful reunion after a parting which had seemed to last for years. Lucy breathed a deep sigh of contentment. It was the profound sense of something having finished, something being at last complete. Now all she wanted was to rest.

Lucy closed her eyes. The softness suffused and surrounded her, flowing over her body like a balmy summer wave. It was as if she was being transported, floating on a sea of forgetfulness, on and on, to the horizon and beyond, and finally to a deep and peaceful sleep.

High overhead, the storm burst across the marsh and the first drop of rain thudded on the surface of the lake. There was an air of dull finality about the sound.

Chapter Twenty-Six

"I'm afraid there's a limit to what we can do in the dark," said the constable, shining his torch out across the ice. "There's a team of men coming over from the village, but the roads will be treacherous in these conditions. Besides, if she has gone under, we'll be too late to save her now."

All around them, the rain was falling with a torrential fury, while overhead the lightning flashed and bathed the lake in a ghastly sheen.

"There!" cried Mrs Latter, pointing to a gaping hole in the ice. "Over to the right! That's where she must have fallen through . . ." The constable shone his torch in the direction she was indicating.

"It's very near to the bank," he retorted. "Tragic, I'd say. I suppose she wanted to get the children off first. Did they tell you what they were doing out there?" Mrs Latter wrung her hands in agitation.

"I-I'm not sure," she replied. "They were so frightened when I found them. Pale as ghosts and so cold. Much longer wandering on the marsh . . . Well," she added, drawing herself up, "it doesn't bear thinking about!"

"Has the doctor seen them?"

"Yes. I left her with them. She said that they were in a state of shock, poor mites. But nothing that a few days' rest couldn't cure. They look such fragile little things. But children are always stronger than you think."

"So they didn't tell you anything?" the constable asked. "Apart from the fact that their aunt had been drowned?"

Mrs Latter coughed nervously. There was an awkward pause.

"They were so scared, you see . . .," she began. "I don't suppose they knew what they were saying . . ." Her voice trailed off beneath the sound of the falling rain. The constable waited in silence. Mrs Latter took a deep breath and carried on.

"They kept talking about their aunt trying to kill them . . . poison them, I think they said . . . and then something about a knife . . . It was probably the shock," she concluded, half apologetically.

"I see," said the constable. "Do you know anything about this woman, Mrs Latter?"

"I only met her once," she replied. "I came over a few days after they moved in. Just to introduce myself and see if they needed anything. She was polite enough, but very detached. Said she wasn't really up to meeting people – that she was still getting over her brother's death . . ." She stopped as, high above their heads, the wind screamed out in shrill lament and the thunder reverberated across the marsh.

"And how was he killed?" persisted the constable,

raising his voice above the clamour of the storm. Mrs Latter paused and waited for the noise to die away.

"In a car accident," she answered. "With his wife. That's how the children came to be with their aunt. I remember her saying something about not wanting to stay in the family home. Too many memories of her brother, she said. So they moved here. Although I can't imagine why she should have chosen somewhere so remote."

"And do you know where they came from?" the constable persevered.

"Not exactly," Mrs Latter responded. "But I gathered from what she said that the family was very wealthy. Maybe even titled a few years back. So it must have been strange for the children moving to a place like this. Lonely too, I should think." She glanced back towards the house as another flash of lightning cut a jagged path across the sky. The windows were dark and horribly empty, like sightless eyes staring out across the marsh, while the walls glowed a sickly yellow in the garish light. Mrs Latter shuddered and pulled her coat tight around her.

"You know, the funny thing is, they were due to move out in a few days' time." She turned her gaze swiftly back towards the lake.

"What will happen to the children?" inquired the constable. Mrs Latter sighed.

"There's another sister. On the mother's side. I rang her up to tell her what had happened. She sounded very anxious. Very concerned. Wanted to come and pick the children up straight away. So I imagine she'll look after them." Mrs Latter gazed steadily out across the ice. "Might've been better if she'd had them from the start . . .," she muttered, under her breath.

"And did the children say anything else that you remember?" asked the constable. Mrs Latter hesitated.

"No. Not really," she replied. She felt her face burning in the cold night air and the man's eyes, peering at her through the darkness. While all around the wind and the rain swirled in a terrible torment.

"Could we talk somewhere else?" demanded Mrs Latter hurriedly. The man smiled indulgently. To their left a large solitary willow stood silhouetted against the sky.

"Over there!" she cried, heading for the shelter of the tree. The man obediently followed. Above their heads the branches writhed and twisted in the agony of the storm, but the trunk was smooth and firm as Mrs Latter leant on it for support.

"Now, where were we?" the constable began. His face, drained of its normal colour, gleamed hollow and ravenous in the torchlight.

"You were asking about the children," said Mrs Latter. "Whether they told me anything else."

"And?" prompted the man. There was a silence and a curious laugh.

"They did tell me things," she said at last. "But whether they're worth repeating . . . and whether you'll believe them . . ."

"Do you believe them, Mrs Latter?"

"Maybe," she replied. "I don't know." Again she sensed his eyes, resting inquisitively upon her face.

"They said there were strange things happening in the house," she began. "Noises. Doors opening and being knocked on. That sort of thing." Mrs Latter stopped. The man coughed awkwardly and the darkness hung heavy with his disbelief. She decided to press on.

135

"They said something about a brooch, appearing as if from nowhere. And a clock – a huge grandfather clock – falling over of its own accord."

The torch flashed suddenly in her face. Mrs Latter blinked and turned away. Not far from her feet, a bough stretched from the bank out across the lake. She wondered if it had fallen in the storm.

"Were they frightened?" asked the constable. Mrs Latter thought she could detect a note of mockery in his voice.

"Yes. At first," she answered. "But then they started to feel that whatever it was, it was trying to help. It was on their side so to speak." She waited while the constable cleared his throat.

"But did they *see* anything, Mrs Latter?"

"No. At least . . ." she hesitated, afraid of incurring his scorn. "The boy didn't see anything. But, just before they left, Emily thought she saw a girl. A young girl. About twelve years old."

"And this . . . this girl," continued the man. "Have you any idea who she might be?"

Mrs Latter gave an involuntary shudder as a drop of rain ran like an icy finger down her back.

"I-I wouldn't have," she stuttered. "But Emily described her so exactly. It couldn't be anyone else . . ." She swallowed hard but the lump in her throat remained. She breathed deep but the breath came in short sharp bursts. "Ten years ago," she started, "a young girl lived here. Just her and her brother and her mother. The father had left not long after they moved in. The three of them were very close . . ."

"And you think this could be the girl who was spotted?" asked the constable. Mrs Latter nodded. The man frowned.

136

"But it could hardly be the same girl, Mrs Latter," declared the man. "After all, if this was ten years ago, she would have to be twenty-two by now." Mrs Latter closed her eyes and leant harder against the tree.

"You don't understand," she answered. "She didn't leave ten years ago. She was killed."

There was an embarrassed silence. The man shifted uneasily on his feet. "I don't think I quite follow you, Mrs Latter . . ."

"She was drowned on the lake," Mrs Latter explained. "Her and her brother together. It was just about this time of year. Their mother had bought them some skates as an early Christmas present. People had always skated on the lake. There had never been any accidents before."

"I see," said the constable, with obvious misgiving.

"But the ice was too thin. Just like tonight. The girl went under trying to save her brother. Of course, the mother blamed herself. She was so distraught when they brought their bodies up. She had them carried to the bedroom and left them there for days. She couldn't bear the thought of burying them, you see. They were such lovely children. So vibrant and alive. It was hard to believe that they could die."

The constable stamped his feet against the cold. He was well aware that Mrs Latter was suffering from the effects of an over-active imagination. But then his job demanded a certain amount of tact.

"So what happened to the mother?" he asked at last, in an effort to placate her.

"She moved away," replied Mrs Latter. "Couldn't bear to live in the house, but couldn't bear to sell it either. So she rented it out – with the sole proviso that nothing in the children's room was touched. As far as

I know, it's exactly the same as they left it – all those years ago."

"Well – she'll be getting some new tenants now," rejoined the man, trying to change the subject.

"No," responded Mrs Latter. "She passed away last week – finally died of a broken heart. That's why the children and their aunt were moving out. The house is going up for sale."

The constable noted, with some relief, that there were several lights approaching from the marsh.

"The men have arrived!" he declared triumphantly. "We'd better go and meet them."

"You know, we haven't had snow since then. Not for ten years. Not until now," Mrs Latter mused.

"Ah!" replied the constable, glancing cheerfully around. "But look, Mrs Latter. It's all melting!" and pulling his helmet tight upon his head, he marched off towards the gate. The ground squelched beneath his stalwart tread. These country folk – they were so superstitious! The constable was proud of his common sense.

So was it merely curiosity which prompted him to ask? Or was it the chill blast which, sweeping him from the house, seemed to encircle him and close upon his heart? He stopped and turned.

"Those children," he began. "The ones who died . . . What were their names?"

Mrs Latter gazed at him uncertainly through the darkness.

"Lucy and Hugh," she said.